A FLASH OF
WORDS

Thanks for the support. Enjoy!

M. R. Wal

Published by Scout Media
Copyright 2019
ISBN: 978-0-9979485-4-7

Cover and story header designs by **Amy Hunter**

Visit: **www.ScoutMediaBooksMusic.com**
For more information on each author and all volumes
in the *Of Words* series.

Table of Contents

THE CALIFORNIAN
JM AMES

Cecilia kicked shut the door to Room 630 and slammed the hotel keys on the adjacent table so hard it made the bathroom door across the room rattle in its frame.

"Welcome to the Californian!" muffled voices down the corridor taunted, followed by high-pitched gales of laughter.

She raised her middle finger high at the disembodied voices before flicking on the kitchenette and main lights.

Jerks! Why would they let transients sleep in the hallway? And what rundown fleabag of a hotel still uses these old-school metal keys?

She rolled her luggage to the bed and flung herself onto her back with a sigh. Her reflection from the mirrored ceiling glowered at her with annoyed exhaustion. Stains of unknown origin mottled the bedspread.

Real classy, Californian. So glad the airline put me up in this dump.

She was *supposed* to be on her way to Puerto Vallarta to relax and drink poolside with the rest of her girls. Cecilia wasn't flush like they were, so she had to take a red-eye flight from Winslow, with a layover in LAX. A suspicious package had forced the evacuation of the airport while she was between planes, and all flights were canceled until they got the all-clear. After giving the airline clerk a hefty earful for the inconvenience, she finally conceded to the delay.

"I think I know just the perfect place for you, ma'am," he had said. She could hear the smug cockiness in his voice.

At least they offered free accommodations, but Cecilia was pretty sure she'd prefer sleeping in the terminal to this skid-row relic.

As if in response to her thoughts, the main room's light flashed, then died with a faint pop, converting the room into a dimly lit funhouse of shadows.

Yep, this is how my day is going. What was it that creepy kid Don at the front desk had said? 'You can check out any time you like?' I wonder if it is too early now …

Her reflection peered down at her with a darkness she wasn't wearing.

What the—

A soft thud from the bathroom banished all thoughts and irritation. She leapt to her feet, ears straining. A nearly inaudible hiss of *something* sliding along the bathroom floor, raising goose bumps on her arms and prickling the hairs on the back of her neck. Her bladder threatened to release the pressure that had been building since the flight.

Cecilia grabbed a lamp from the bedside table and crept to the bathroom door. Her knees wobbled and threatened to buckle. She pursed her lips to smother the chattering of her teeth. As she was almost upon it, she heard the shower curtain slide open. Her insides filled with ice water, and she yelped in fright before she could stop herself. A floorboard in the bathroom groaned under some shifting weight. A trickle of urine escaped her bladder and warmed her inner thigh.

The bathroom door burst open, and a screaming figure charged from the dark with a baton-like weapon raised above their head. The shower curtain rod smashed onto her hand and knocked the lamp to the ground, where it cracked in half. Cecilia screamed in agony, rage, and terror and shoved her assailant back into the barely lit bathroom. Her adversary fell on their back with a grunt.

Cecilia charged at the person, and a stomp-kick to her soiled groin greeted her. She collapsed to her knees, gasping in pain. Still lying on the ground, her attacker swung again with the rod, but this time, Cecilia grabbed it with both hands and wrenched it from their grasp. She held it vertically, raised it above her head, and thrust down with all her weight.

She stood and flipped on the light switch. The body trembled and shook. Blood flowed from where the rod protruded from the attacker's eye socket.

Cecilia crept closer to the woman on the floor and shrieked when she recognized the broken face as her own.

Her knees finally gave way, and she fainted, collapsing into the fetal position alongside her gurgling doppelganger.

She opened her eyes some time later and winced at the throbbing pain in the back of her head. The bathroom was dark again. Cecilia pulled herself up and shuffled to the light switch, not lifting her feet, to avoid tripping over the body.

The bathroom looked immaculate, as if housekeeping had just left—no body, no blood, and the shower curtain was back in its proper place, undisturbed and clean.

Am I losing my mind?

Her swollen, bruised hand and aching crotch didn't seem to think so.

Light clanking and clicking at the front door signaled someone was entering the room. Cecilia flipped off the light and eased the bathroom door closed. The front door slammed shut, and Cecilia covered mouth to keep from screaming.

Keys hit the table. She heard people talking in the hallway—voices, but no distinct words. Light footsteps stepped across the room, then silence.

Cecilia had been leaning toward the door and started to lose her balance. She put her hand on the door to steady herself and realized her mistake when she heard a sharp intake of breath from the room.

Panicked, she shuffled backward to the shower, then, as quietly as she could, detached the curtain rod from the wall and slid it off the curtain. She raised it above her head and crept back to the door.

A soft cry on the other side made her jump. Cecilia flung open the door.

Another body double! What the hell is going on?

She charged, screaming, the rod raised high above her head. She swung hard and knocked the lamp from the *other* Cecilia's hand, where it tumbled to the floor and cracked in half ...

***

For more information on this author, visit: jm-ames.com

EARTH II ⚡
ALANAH ANDREWS ⚡

Rose donned the clunky spacesuit and pressed the button that would release the first of the doors guarding the precious environment of the base from the arid air outside. Stepping through, the door closed with a slight *whuff*, and the second button popped out of its cavity abruptly. Rose hesitated.

Don't leave the base.

The message had been drilled into Rose's mind since she was a small child.

Don't ever leave the base.

She knew that there was only a slim chance of success. Less, according to her father, who referred to it as a suicide mission. But when she asked him for an alternative, he had come up short. They had all come up short.

One working oxygen tank left. One volunteer. Rose tried not to tremble as she pressed her gloved hand against the release button and the second door slid back, revealing the shadowy and treacherous terrain outside.

Her mind protested as she took that first step out and onto the red-tinged ground. She was leaving the one place that had provided her with everything she needed for her entire life. Recirculated air and water; plants grown beneath complex lighting systems; wind-generated power to run the necessities. And it wasn't only her—the base had sustained this small offshoot of the human race for nine generations.

Until now.

Until a vital component of the air-purification system had started to wear out and crumble. Until staying at the base meant death as certainly as leaving it. Twelve months. That was the estimate given by the engineers, give or take.

Rose sighed as she worked out her destination. The base was nestled within a large valley surrounded by uneven peaks, which protected them from the majority of the harsh weather. She set her sights on the closest hill rising from the ground to the north of the base. She was counting on being able to see the site of the original landing from the top of that hill. The Party wouldn't have left them stranded; they would have planned for a critical moment such as this.

When she thought of the Party, Rose touched the front of her helmet briefly as she had done all her life and muttered, "For the good of the people." Her voice sounded hollow within the clunky dome.

As Rose trudged towards the hills, she thought of all that she had been taught about that monumental moment. They had landed on a Sunday after plunging through space for seven days. Or was it seven months? The specifics weren't important, thought Rose—what mattered was the Party and what they had done for the people of Earth.

She—along with all of the residents living in the base—had the Party to thank for their existence. When Earth descended into chaos and the fighting began, the Party had looked to the stars for a solution. Overpopulation was rampant, and nuclear war was likely to turn the Earth's surface into an uninhabitable wasteland.

Not unlike the surface she was walking on now, thought Rose wryly.

A small group of select people had escaped the doomed world and fled to a new planet. Earth II, it was nostalgically named. That was nine generations ago. The founding members had long since perished, but their laws remained strong. Don't leave the base. Don't breathe the outside air. Two children per family maximum. Don't waste resources. The Party is good.

The Party is good.

Rose sometimes looked up at the stars, wondering which of the glowing specks was the original Earth. In the best-case scenario, she would be able to contact Earth from the spaceship and have them send a rescue team. Party lore stated that one day they would be able to return to a cleansed world. Surely nine generations since the nuclear war would be enough for Earth to have recovered? Rose longed to set foot on the planet of their origin and finally smell the flower that she had been wistfully named after.

In the worst-case scenario, where Earth had not yet recuperated or the communication systems had been broken, Rose hoped that at least she would find some backup supplies. Additional tools, if she was lucky. A spare valve, if she was really lucky. It was vital to repair that ventilation system if they were going to survive for a tenth generation.

Rose reached the base of the hill and looked up. It was higher than it had first appeared. The innocent lights blinking on her oxygen tank told her she had an hour left. She hoped it would be enough.

But as she lifted her foot to begin her ascent, something at the foot of the hill a few hundred metres to her right caught her attention. A movement. The land was always a shadowy wasteland, but as the wind blew past in fits and gusts, something at the base of the hill had rolled over; she was certain of it.

She looked up at the hill and then changed her mind. Turning right, she hurried along the ground in the direction of the thing-that-had-moved.

She knew it couldn't be an animal; the perpetual gloom and toxins in the air meant that no living thing could thrive outside. Even the hardiest of plants struggled to find nutrients in the barren ground. Perhaps, the thing-that-had-moved was a bit of wreckage from the landing, Rose thought hopefully. As she approached the small object, Rose stared in open fascination.

It was about the size of a boot, and it reminded her of the drinking vessels at the base, but, unlike those containers, it had a sealed top. She picked it up awkwardly in her gloved hands and studied the half-worn label. "Coca-Cola," she read aloud. The object was made of some sort of transparent flexible material. She looked closer. "Made in Australia."

Rose frowned. The container must have been made on Earth, so what was it doing here? Was the shuttle nearby? She needed a higher vantage point, but as she went to climb the hill, a quiet crunching sound came from beneath her foot. Bending down, Rose clawed at the dirt to reveal three more of the containers huddled together beneath the ground.

Was the entire hill made of these strange flexible bottles? Rose's thoughts swirled together in confusion, and she started to feel sick. Things weren't making any sense.

Rose began to climb quickly. Her breath grew short, and she didn't need to check her oxygen metre to know that time was running out. Finally, Rose stood at the top of the hill and surveyed the land around her.

There were more hills beyond the one she was standing on. Some were sprouting metallic objects like a bizarre forest she might have seen encased within the pages of a picture book. Beyond the hills, the land stretched out—flat and sandy. Disappointment bloomed in her belly. There was no spaceship anywhere that she could see—no debris or hole where the craft had settled onto the surface of the planet either.

And then her eyes were drawn towards something far away in the distance, to the west of the base. She gasped and stared uncomprehendingly at the strange towering structures of that distant, ruined city.

***

For more information on this author, visit: alanahandrews.com

JUNK
ADAM BENNETT

Alen stared at the junk sitting on the living room table.

Jenny had gone and gotten more. He'd said he was done last night, but maybe she hadn't realised he meant it this time.

One more night wouldn't hurt.

One more last hurrah before giving it up for good.

And this time, he would make sure that Jenny knew he was done. It was for her own good too. If he got clean, he could help her get clean as well. It was going to be okay.

After another moment's hesitation, he reached for the hit Jenny was offering him and soon slumbered in blissful numb warmth, silky smooth over all the jagged edges of the world.

He woke covered in his own piss.

Enough was enough.

The first two days were itchy as hell, waking every fifteen minutes, now hot, suddenly cold, flop sweats, and sustained dry retching minutes after his stomach's meagre contents hit his shoes.

The erections were the worst problem. Ejaculating every ten minutes because he bumped against something was pure hell.

And then, on the third day, Jenny scored again.

"What the fuck were you thinking? You know what I'm going through right now. You're a fucking bitch!"

"Well excuse me for being proud of your two days sober and wanting to give you a little relief. Jesus, you'd think I'd fucking killed someone!"

Alen backed down. "I'm sorry. I'm on edge. If you were trying to be nice ... I'm sorry."

It took another three days for him to work up the courage to quit again, and this time, he managed a week before he walked into the living room to find Jenny in the middle of a hit.

"What the fuck!"

"What?"

"You can't do that around me!"

"I didn't think you were here."

"You keep doing this! Are you trying to sabotage me on purpose?"

Jenny started crying. "You are such an asshole to me. I don't know why I bother. Just because you can't handle your shit doesn't mean I should have to suffer all the time. Just fuck off."

"Jesus fuck!" Alen sat beside her and put an arm around her. "I'm sorry. I'm so on edge. Give me that. I'll be less of an asshole. Sorry."

After a week, Alen once more attempted to quit.

It lasted the afternoon.

"Seriously? Are you really doing this right now? Today?"

Jenny didn't respond.

"I asked if you were seriously going to get high on the first day of me trying to quit, right here in the kitchen."

She said nothing.

"I asked you a question!"

Jenny turned and leveled a flat gaze. She spoke, barely raising her voice above a whisper. "I've had it with this, you fucking drug-addict scum. No, shut the fuck up and listen to me for once. Are you listening? Good. None of this is real, you fucking moron. It's all in your head. *I* am not an addict. *You* are the only addict here. I have never, and *will* never touch that shit that you are holding in your hand right now. I'm sick to fucking death of you walking into a room where I am sitting peacefully, lighting up a bowl of that junk, blowing the smoke all over the room, and then yelling at me for ruining your sobriety. The fucking shrink told me to let you live in your little fantasy world. He said pulling you out of it could be seriously bad news, but I've had enough of this shit. You are a sick scumbag fuck, and I'm goddamn done!" Jenny stood, pulled a packed suitcase from beneath the kitchen table, and rolled it out the front door.

Alen watched her leave, perplexed. He looked down at the brown liquid rolling within the dirty glass pipe in his hand and shook his head in rage. As the door closed behind her, he shouted, "Don't forget to take your junk, you crazy bitch! *I* don't fucking want it!"

***

For more information on this author, visit:
amazon.com/author/a.alexander

A FAMILY THING
ELDRED BIRD

"Lower the drawbridge!" Owen skittered across the low-hanging tree limb and latched onto a dry twig. He snapped it off and waved it in the air like the mighty sword Excalibur.

"Get out of my castle and don't come back! No? Then prepare to fight!" He lunged forward, swinging his weapon at the branches blocking his path across the arboreal bridge. With each thrust and parry, he advanced, vanquishing foes. When he reached the end of the limb, the brave swordsman leapt to the ground, rolled in the grass, and sprang back to his feet. He spun around on one foot and kicked at the air.

"Into the moat with you, scoundrel! The crocodiles will finish you off!" Owen continued his advance through the autumn leaves—running, tumbling, and plunging his wooden blade into the bushes and tall grass. People driving by on the narrow country lane appeared oblivious to the battle raging just off the pavement—Owen was equally oblivious to their presence.

He continued to cut a swath through the invisible army until he reached the driveway, then doubled back toward the house where his father stood peering out of the big picture window. Owen stopped, grinned, and waved at him before running back to the shade of the large tree.

"There's something wrong with that boy."

"Why do you say that?" Owen's mother looked up from her book. "What's he doing?"

"He's running around the yard yelling and poking things with a stick."

"So?"

"So, the neighbors are going to think he's crazy."

"He's not crazy, dear, he's just playing."

"He's talking to himself again. Why can't he just play videogames like the other kids?"

"He's not like the other kids."

"That's what I'm saying. He's not normal."

"Okay, I guess it's time I told you." She closed her book, set it aside, and patted the couch cushion next to her. "You'll probably want to sit down for this."

"That sounds ominous." Owen's father melted onto the couch and faced his wife. "There really is something wrong with the boy?"

"Yes." She took his hands and stared deep into his eyes. "It's genetic … something that runs in my family. My father had it, I have it, and I'm afraid I passed it along to our son."

"Is it serious?"

She lowered her head. "Very."

"Can it be cured?"

"No, it's something he'll have to learn to live with."

He gripped her hands tighter. "What is it?"

She shook her head. "I don't really know how to tell you this."

"Just say it straight out. I can take it."

"Okay, here goes nothing. Owen has …" She took a deep breath. "An imagination!"

***

For more information on this author, visit:
facebook.com/EldredBirdAuthor

THE WAIL OF A SIREN
SHIVANI CHATTERJEE

Splash!

And another sailor jumps overboard.
The moonlit waves toss him like a ragdoll; the rocky shore
mangles his limbs.
My soul turns the color of his blood
As he paints the ocean red.
His body will sink into the navy-blue depths,
The frothy white surf is soon to be the sole trace of his existence.

I can't help what I am. I can't help my thirst for a man's blood;
As ship upon ship sail close to the Island of the Sirens,
My unquenched thirst lights me up like red-hot flames.
I am bound in servitude to my lineage,
A lineage of tortured souls whose only respite is taking a life.
I do not want to be this way, I didn't choose to be a murderer.
But my voice is its own master, and it listens to none.

Slowly at first, I feel a warm tickle at my heart,
And I open my mouth as sweet, sweet music pours out.
It feels good, this warmth in my heart,
And the men stop what they're doing and listen.
The smarter among them cover their ears.
The fire is getting hotter, and it's spreading through my body;
A creature of the water! I feel like I'm consumed in flames!
And as the pain worsens, my cries get higher and clearer
And the sailors crane their necks to hear more.
More, more, more. I sound beautiful, I am beautiful,

I am enchanting, alluring … a monster.

Deep inside lives a scared little girl
Innocent, pure. Lonely.
Each time a sailor plunges into the navy and white, she dies a little;
All she ever wanted was love.
A snake is not evil for it bites
A scorpion not cruel for it stings
It is their nature to wound, to hurt.
It is my nature to sing.

Now I see him, the captain of the ship!
The leader of his sailors, the man in navy and white.
The pale blue light of the moon illuminates his chestnut hair.
He bites his lip, concentration carving lines in his face
As he tries to ignore my haunting song.
He knows what happens to men like him,
Led astray, lured to death.

Captain, you deserve to live!
My voice overpowers the little girl within.
It is a plaintive, melodious cry of passion, of desperation.
It's irresistible. He cannot help but listen—
But I do not want to see him die!
Captain! Turn back!
Captain, come closer …
Captain, cover your ears!
Captain, listen to me …

For a moment our eyes meet,
And the man in navy and white removes his hands from his ears.
Stop! Don't listen to me!

But my voice does not obey me, and my song carries pain my heart cannot bear.
The fire within sparks up and scorches my soul
As I lie glowing on the shore.
My song is the wail of an anguished heart,
For beneath the lustrous, shimmering waves
Lies darkness.
Captain, what are you doing?
I am devoured by the flames as they pour out of my eyes.
He walks towards the railing.
Captain, don't do it!
It's inevitable.

Splash.

THE CONSEQUENCES OF GRIEF
LOZZI COUNSELL

The wind is cold against my body as I reach into my pocket and twiddle the small pill between my fingers. The stars are twinkling up above; although, their brightness is only dim. It doesn't matter though because I know my way to this part of the field, whether I am led by sunlight or moonlight.

I lie down, flattening the grass beneath me—there are daisies, buttercups, and even tulips here.

I slide the pill out of my pocket and hold it in my wrinkly palm. Doctors call it the Final Goodbye Pill. Known as the biggest breakthrough in science for many years, it allows grieving individuals the chance to say goodbye after a loss by bringing back the spirit of their loved one for a short time. But as everyone knows, all pills have side-effects.

After the sudden death of my daughter, I was so distraught that my wife had begged me to see a psychiatrist. I was one of the first to try out the Final Goodbye Pill, but for me, one goodbye was and will never be enough. How do you say goodbye to your own child, the one person you thought would outlive you? I never got to see her graduate school, let alone get the chance to walk her down the aisle. I thought that one day she would cry at my funeral. I wasn't meant to go to hers. But everyone has their price, and my life savings were enough to cover the cost of a small bag of the pills.

My hands begin to shake as I look at the pill one last time before popping it in my mouth. I have now lost count of the amount I have taken over the past three months since Martha's death.

"Please don't take the pill!" my wife Claudia had begged, her hand wrapped tightly around my wrist. We were standing in the hallway of our house, surrounded by memories of what was. The house hasn't changed at all since we lost Martha; her denim jacket is still hanging on the banister at the bottom of the stairs, and her bike is still leaning against the garden fence. Neither of us have even ventured into her bedroom since the horrible accident, and I can imagine it now—her bed all creased from where she last slept in it, her clothes folded up at the bottom of her bed ready for the morning.

"I've lost Martha as well!" Claudia had wept, her brown hair now streaked with grey kept up in a bun, her eyes bloodshot from tears. "You can't keep putting me through this; I don't know how much more I can take."

I hesitated, just for a second, but a second was enough for her to loosen her grip. I had shaken her off and fled out of the front door. She hadn't tried to run after me or even call out my name. I clutched at my stinging wrist; I had forgotten how strong she was, since we'd both become so emotionally weak.

They say that time heals, but time hasn't put a plaster on my grieving heart and picked my body up off the floor. I draw in a deep breath, shut my eyes, and wait for the pill to take effect. I am used to the process now. First the tingling sensation begins, until my whole body becomes numb from my toes to my fingertips, and after that I ...

Blackout.

I wake from what feels like a nap and scrunch up my fingers and toes, making sure that the tingling is gone, along with the numbness. It is still very late at night and everything looks the same as before; although, the moon seems higher up and somehow bigger and brighter.

"Hello, Dad. I knew you'd come back!"

I turn to my left and smile. Martha is sitting on the ground next to me, a tiara of daisies entwined in her long blonde hair that lies in waves over her pale shoulders. She grabs my hand in hers; her skin is surprisingly warm, considering the chilly air.

"Where's Mum?" Martha grins, hopefully.

"She couldn't make it, darling. You know she would be here if she could," I reply robotically with the line I have been rehearsing in my head over and over again on the journey here. I pull her close to my chest, holding her. I can sense the disappointment swimming across her face as I kiss her freckled forehead gently.

The next few minutes are spent together, just like we used to do. I tell her made-up stories about how happy me and her mum are, and she tells me about what she's been doing with her time since we last met, including how she had made the beautiful daisy tiara in her hair. But I know the pill doesn't last. Once again, I can see her body begin to turn to a blur in front of my eyes, and I know that our time is up.

"No," I cry, trying to cling on to her. "I'm not ready!"

"It's okay, Dad," she whispers, stroking my cheek gently.

I wrap my arms around her tightly, somehow hoping that my strong arms can prevent the inevitable. I squeeze my eyes shut and refuse to let go until I can't feel her there anymore. My arms loosen, and I drop to the ground with a sigh of helplessness.

"Why?" I whimper, curling my legs up beneath my body. "Why?" I begin to shout the word louder, knowing no one can hear me and no one can reply to my pain.

It is now that I notice the aging to my body. I want to claw at the ground in anger, but my arthritic fingers prevent such movements, and I can feel aches and pains where I've never had them before. I try to stand, but my hips and legs have lost their strength, so instead I crawl over to a nearby tree stump and pull myself up, using it as support. Every step I take is a challenge as I shuffle closer to home. I know that my body can't take it anymore. I need to stop doing this. I need to put Claudia first now.

The door is locked when I get home, and the lights are off. I am excited at the thought of seeing Claudia's face light up and beam with pride when I admit what a fool I have been lately and how I have been taking her for granted. I fiddle around in my coat pocket until I find my house keys.

I flick the light switch on, but to my surprise, I am greeted by a cold, empty house. All the photos of our once happy family are placed facing down, and everything of my wife's is gone. I collapse against the wall. With my head in my hands, I rock back and forth in silence, tears running down my face. I once had everything, and now I have lost it all. I once had a beautiful child and a beautiful wife to share my life with, and now one is dead, and the other has left me.

I look up at the mirror on the wall and take my appearance in properly for the first time in months. My hair had once been full and black, but now it is white and thinning. My once bright eyes are now grey, lifeless, and sunken. My once athletic body is full of aches and pains, and my hands have a permanent shake to them. Yet I'm only thirty-seven. What have I done to myself?

I pull the remaining pills out of my pocket and drop them onto the floor in front of me; there are three left. By now, my body is that of an eighty-seven-year-old. The three pills would add another fifteen years onto that to make me …

I pick up the first and swallow it, feeling the same tingling sensation that I have already felt today. I don't stop there though as I swallow a second pill and then a third.

I smile to myself as I catch a glimpse of the all-so-familiar long blonde hair entwined with a tiara of daisies, knowing I won't have to leave her this time.

***

For more information on this author, visit:
facebook.com/LozziAuthor

HUT, HUT, BANG
CURTIS A. DEETER ⚡

Bang. Your last night in paradise comes crashing down.

Is it a car crash? Or was someone shot? It doesn't happen often on your side of paradise, but it's possible. It happens on other sides. Maybe the world's ending. Maybe it's all already over.

You have the music up—some EDM jam with a nondescript female vocalist. By the sounds she's making, she's enjoying whatever's being done to her within the privacy of those woodgrain Klipsch towers. You're moving to the waves of her ecstasy while riding your own. Every night's a party, and what they say is completely wrong: it *is* still popping, especially if it happens every night.

Wood splinters. Cheap hinges burst. Someone in the kitchen screams and spills half-cooked ramen noodles down the front of the dishwasher. Broth seeps in through the cracks and crevices. It'll take months to clean up the remnants.

You're with Alexandria or Rhiannen or Kylie; it's hard to remember which flavor you like best when you've had them all. She's doing her best impression of a busy elevator, and you don't even care if the cable snaps.

Titans in black file in, Kevlar monsters flailing their AR15 arms. They don't say *hut, hut, hut, hut* like you imagined they would; blame Hollywood for that. Or John Landis—whoever you find first. Instead, they spit lava and rough you up. Leroy lands on a half-eaten Taco Bell burrito. Jacques spills his first Busch Light all over the socks your grandma knitted for you. A lamp breaks, leaving only the strobe light in the corner. The monsters move toward you through endless wormholes of light.

You realize you're still hanging out of your pants, but that's okay. It's gotten you out of trouble before, why not now? Remember that time you got caught sneaking into your ex's house? Her mother had been so upset with you until you let Willy free. She told you how lonely she was while she cooked you beef bourguignon.

Hollow, polarized eyes stare into your soul. He needs a Tic Tac—this monster whose breath fogs the inside of his mask—but you'd incite a riot of brutality for saying so. He's the Death Bringer, so you smile. Green crystals from the spliff you just finished cling to your teeth.

"Wanna die, funny man?" the Death Bringer says.

Something cold and steel sticks its tongue to your temple. Out the corner of your eye, you can already see your gray matter splattered on the smoke-yellowed wall.

"Do you want to fucking take that ride?"

It wouldn't be the weirdest ride you've taken. There was that one time at What's-his-name's house—Carlito or Mateo or Chris or something. You psilocybin slid right up to him after everyone else had left and strapped yourself in. You never told anyone. You never even thought about it until just now.

Someone changes the song to Cyndi Lauper. You know immediately by the patterns of the synth and because the monsters in black are laughing. They're laughing and talking about the Browns or their wives as they tear pages from books, topple your dressers, and eat the pizza in your fridge. Your stomach growls. You shiver because the cold Busch Light is still bleeding onto your foot, and your sock is absorbing it.

Is it as cold as the cabin up north? You think hard on it, remembering the times spent opening and closing Vs with your skis, drinking Bailey's-spiked hot cocoa in the hot tub, and answering the tremolo of the loon at midnight, but you know you can't compare the two coldnesses. They're polar opposites.

The Death Bringer picks you up by your arms like you're a

pig on a spit. He tosses you onto the couch and lines up three of his biggest friends to take cracks at you. They make fun of your peach-fuzz face. They jab your exposed genitalia with the butts of their guns. They gesture at Alexandria or Rhiannen or Kylie, making a popping sound when they draw their thumbs from their drooling mouths.

She looks to you, mascara streaked down her cheeks, and curses you. This is all your fault. You've never wanted her more now that you know you'll never have her again.

They're still buzzing around like a mob of great black wasps. You know if you bug them, they'll only turn their stingers on you, but you have to piss, smoke a cigarette, or bury your head in the dirt out back.

"Found it," one of the wasps says to the Death Bringer, holding a six-ounce bag of Afghan Kush in front of him like it's a stick of dynamite. "Some cash too."

The cash is for textbooks. The weed is for having a good time. *It's not like it's crack or something,* you think as you're about to crack up. The Death Bringer has smelled your stuff, and, by the raising of his upper lip, he likes what he smells. At least someone's going to have a good time later.

Leroy, still belly down on a burrito, salsa verde smeared across his cardigan, coughs or sneezes or breathes too hard. That part is still a blur. All you know is one second you're biting your lip as the Death Bringer is licking tetrahydrocannabinol off the pad of his pinky, and the next second the room erupts in screams for mercy. The acoustics aren't great for this sort of thing, and the shot rings in your ears for months afterward.

A week later, when you're alone and packing the single suitcase of the things you really need from that apartment, you find a piece of Leroy's brain behind the Kolsch speakers. You think maybe it's bubblegum, but you've never been more wrong in your life.

A voice calls from the parking lot. Your mom honks the horn of her Lexus. She's on edge and forgot her happy pills at home. If she doesn't get back there fast, she is literally going to lose it. You haven't told her what happened here last week or why she hasn't seen your cute best friend for a few days. You're not sure how she'd take it, other than calling you a druggy or a hippy before drowning herself in peach SKYY vodka.

Bang.

Don't worry, the world hasn't ended. Well, yours has. It's just the car door slamming outside. It's just your mother rapping her fist on the front door. It's just the thrilling climax of the Tarantino movie blaring next door. It's just Leroy's head exploding like a watermelon at a Gallagher show.

***

For more information on this author, visit: curtisadeeter.com

LITTLE WHITE POODLE
WILLIAM G. EDWARDS

"Slow down, George!" Seventy-three-year-old Martha griped as they rounded the corner on a winding Michigan highway through the Hiawatha National Forest.

He tapped the brake and adjusted the speed on the cruise control. George looked over and smiled at Martha's frail face. After forty-six years of marriage, her mind was slowly disappearing due to Alzheimer's, and it scared him. It scared him more than the two combat tours he did in Vietnam. She was his life and stood by his side through war and the seven years he had spent drowning out the memories with alcohol. Now it was his turn to be there for her.

Martha sat up and pointed ahead at a small white poodle trotting down the side of the highway. "George, watch out for the dog."

George let off the gas and pressed the brake pedal. "I see it."

Martha rolled her window down and smiled as they went by. "She's such a pretty girl."

The poodle, with its little blue eyes and a red bow on its head, glanced up her, then looked away.

With sad eyes, Martha looked over at George. "Pull over, George. We can't leave her out here alone."

George pressed the brake pedal and pulled to the side of the road and stopped.

Martha opened her door and stepped out. She bent down, and the poodle stopped ten feet away and stared at her. "Hi, sweetie! Are you lost?"

The little poodle lowered its head and took three steps back. Martha put out her hand—"Don't be afraid"—but the poodle turned and trotted down the embankment toward the tree line thirty feet away. She stopped next to a tall red maple tree, looked back, and whimpered, then disappeared into the dark forest.

"She's scared, George! See if you can get her."

George walked around the back of the car and looked down the embankment. It was steep, and the grass was wet from an earlier rain. He looked back at Martha and saw the worried look on her face, then looked back down the wet embankment. He took a deep breath and started toward the forest.

When he reached the tree line, the poodle peeked its head out from behind a large tree six feet away. George stepped forward. "Come here girl!" he said with a soft voice, but she stepped back behind the tree.

George took a couple steps, tripped over a branch, and landed on his knees with his hands out in front of him.

The poodle stepped out from behind the tree, cocked its head to the side, and watched George push himself up.

Martha put her hands to her mouth. "Are you all right, George?"

George brushed the dirt off his hands and knees. "I'm fine. I tripped over a branch."

"Well, be more careful," she said as she started down the hill. "You're scaring her."

The poodle walked over to George, sat down, and wagged its tail. George reached down with his bleeding hand, and she sniffed his fingers. He picked her up with both hands, cradled her in his arm, and patted her on the head. She wagged her little tail.

"See, girl; I won't hurt you."

"Be careful with her, George."

"She's fine," he said with a laugh as the poodle licked his face. "Let's get you warmed up."

Martha met George at the tree line with a smile.

"Martha, you should have waited by the road. You could have slipped and fell on this slope."

"I'm fine, George. Don't worry about me."

As soon as he stepped out of the woods, she took the dog and snuggled it against her chest. "You're such a cute puppy."

George grabbed Martha's arm and started helping her up the hill. "What the heck!" he said with a puzzled look on his face.

"What's wrong, George?" she asked as she looked up. "Oh my," she exclaimed. "She has friends!"

Eleven poodles, seven white and four black, were sitting on top of the car, staring down at them. Before they had a chance to react, the little poodle in Martha's arms bit into her jugular vein. Martha screamed and threw her to the ground as blood gushed from her neck. The little poodle got up and bit her left ankle as George pulled on her arm to get her up the hill.

The group of poodles jumped off the car and attacked. Eight went for George, taking bites out of his legs in a piranha-like frenzy as he kicked and slapped at them. He got a couple pretty good, but there were too many.

With blood pouring from Martha's neck, her legs buckled under her, and George lost hold of her arm. He reached for her, but the poodles were all over him.

Martha was on her back, slapping and kicking at the crazed poodles until she was too weak to fight. She let out a final scream as they tore into her abdomen and fought over the intestines and organs.

George kept slipping as he made his way up the hill while the poodles kept biting his arms and legs. One got a hold of his neck, and George grabbed him and threw him as hard as he could down the hill. He got the passenger door open and collapsed onto the seat with his legs daggling out.

They continued their attack, jumping in and out of the car in a frenzy. After losing too much blood, George didn't have the strength to fight anymore and lost consciousness. The poodles tore into his abdomen and ripped out his intestines.

They feasted for five minutes, growling and snarling at each other as they staked out their share of the meal. When there wasn't much left, they chewed on the bones and licked the blood off the tan car seat.

They stopped and looked when lights of an approaching car popped over a hill. With their stomachs full and fur soaked in blood, they scattered into the forest.

The car slowed to a crawl as it approached the vehicle and stopped along the opposite side of the highway. A tall, overweight man got out from the driver side, and a slender, blond woman got out on the passenger side.

They walked toward the car. The woman looked in the driver's window and screamed. The man saw George's mutilated legs dangling out the door and Martha's body down the ravine. He backed away yelling, "Get in the car, now!"

They ran to their car, slammed the doors shut, and locked them. The man grabbed his cell phone and dialed 9-1-1. The woman kept screaming, "Oh my God, oh my God," as she frantically squirmed in her seat. She stopped when she saw a dirty, white poodle with a red bow limping out of the woods toward her.

"Oh no, that must be their dog!" she exclaimed as she panickily opened the door. "Come here, girl!"

***

For more information on this author, visit:
www.facebook.com/bill.edwards.547

GOODBYE DADDY
EDDIE HARTSHORN

I love my four-year-old son, I honestly do. But lately, he has scared the crap out of me. He has wedged a deep fear into my soul. Now, before you jump to judging me, allow me to explain. His mother and I welcomed her parents into our home about six years ago. Gramps and Grammy were both in their mid-sixties and not doing so well at taking care of themselves. We did not want them in a senior care facility.

Everything was going fine up to last Tuesday. That evening, I stood at my son's bedroom door and watched him kneel at his bed and pray. "Dear, Lord, please bless Mommy, Daddy, and Grammy." He paused, looked up at the ceiling, then added, "And goodbye to Gramps."

Naturally, I was dumbfounded. Why goodbye to Grandpa? Gramps had been doing fine despite his seldom bouts with dementia. It wasn't like Gramps had been wandering off or anything. Just a few times forgetting why he went into a particular room or where he placed something. And now here was my son, Nolan, saying goodbye to Gramps in a prayer. I wanted to ask why but figured it could wait until morning.

When morning arrived, I heard Grammy scream from behind their bedroom door. Her husband of forty years was dead. It wasn't easy for me to sit at the kitchen table and not drill Nolan. But I held my tongue. My wife, Grammy, and I had to deal with a horrible situation.

The funeral came and went, leaving us with a void. Each night Nolan said his prayers, and each night I stood in his doorway. He said his prayers without a further goodbye, until two nights ago.

"Dear, Lord, please bless Mommy, Daddy, and ..." Nolan went silent and looked up at the ceiling for a good ten seconds. Then he turned his head back to return to his prayer. "And goodbye to Grammy."

Yes, I was thinking the same as you are now. Grammy? Will she be dead in the morning? I watched Nolan climb into bed, pull his covers up to his chest where he turned and smiled at me. "Goodnight, Daddy."

It so happens the next day was Saturday, and I always rise late on the weekends, but not this time. I hardly slept at all. Several times during the night I looked in on Grammy. Each time she was snoring and appeared to be okay.

Come morning, I rushed into her room. She was standing near the foot of the bed half naked. She yelled a few choice words; I apologized and turned to walk out. She sighed and clicked her tongue, in disgust I suppose. Before I cleared her doorway, I heard a loud thump. Yes, the thud was her body landing on the floor. Dead as dead can get.

My wife cried all weekend.

Come Sunday night, I stood in my son's doorway and watched him drop to his knees. "Dear, Lord, please bless Mommy and ..." His eyes turned to the ceiling again. I held my breath. "And goodbye to Daddy."

My knees buckled, my legs shook, my lungs screamed for air even as I sucked in gulps of it. I braced myself against the doorframe and glared at the little fellow as he climbed into bed. He pulled the covers up to his chest where he slowly turned his head and smiled at me.

You little shit, I wanted to say, but the words wouldn't come. Maybe because I suddenly believed he had a connection with God or the Grim Reaper. Either one was more power than I could ever hope to have.

I walked gingerly over to him. My goodness, I didn't want

to upset him in any way whatsoever. "Son, why did you say goodbye to me in your prayer?"

"I don't know, Daddy." Once more he turned his gaze toward the ceiling. "When I looked up there ..." He paused and pointed a finger upward. "I felt I had to say goodbye. That's all."

I took a step back and found myself staring at the ceiling. Painted eggshell white, no cracks, no signs of any supernatural being clinging to his ceiling fan. All looked fine. I scolded myself for even glancing at it. I hugged my son, long and hard, and kissed him goodnight. "I love you, son. I honestly, truly love you! Goodnight."

Come morning, I was surprised and delighted to find myself breathing. Nolan was wrong. Or was he? Grammy hadn't died during the night. She hadn't dropped dead, no pun intended, until after she rose from the bed and began dressing. I pinched myself and looked at my reflection in the dresser mirror. I looked alive, felt alive. I had to be alive!

I kissed my wife and son goodbye and said I had to go to work. My wife was upset with me for not taking bereavement leave for Grammy. I explained I would work a double shift and then get a couple of days off. She did that click of the tongue her mother liked to do and grunted. I kissed her once more on the cheek and hurried out the door. Double shift indeed: I had no plans on returning home until after midnight.

I worked four hours over. The other four hours I killed, pun intended, at Compassionate Bar & Grill. Yes, that was the real name of the joint, and boy was I in need of some compassion.

I didn't drink in excess but sure was tempted. Every so often, I would pinch myself and engage in conversation with the bartender or a nearby patron, hoping I wouldn't die in the middle of a discussion.

I walked through the front door of my house at precisely 12:01 a.m., feeling pretty good in more ways than one. Daddy hadn't died! I was prepared for my wife the moment she met me in the kitchen. "Wow, honey, I sure had a tough day at work. So good to be home." I reached out to pull her to my chest.

She took a step back as if I reeked of alcohol, no doubt I did.

"You had a tough day!" she screamed, throwing her hands up to the air like she was dancing with the Holy Spirit. "You had a tough day? Let me tell you, buster ..." She refilled her lungs. "I have been here dealing with the death of my parents, alone, only to find the mailman lying dead at our doorstep!"

***

For more information on this author, visit:
facebook.com/ShowtimeAtTheGarden/

THE CHROME DREAM
MARLON S. HAYES

Zelda woke me with her singing. I had dreamt of road signs, mile markers, and distant places. I don't know if somehow my dreams entered Zelda's mind using telepathy, but she was singing about highways and byways. I smiled, sleep still clouding my senses. Maybe being married for twenty-eight years had our dreams in perfect harmony. I could see her hazy outline, standing at the sink in the bathroom adjoining our bedroom. Grinning, my hands found my glasses on the nightstand. Sliding them on, my wife came into sharp focus.

Shirtless, clad in a pair of bikini panties, Zelda looked as delicious to me as she had years ago when I saw her naked for the very first time. I could see the changes wrought by years, a thickening in the waist, stretch marks, and a few strands of gray hair. Those were wonderful changes, as far as I was concerned, because they told the tales of our life. Motherhood, contentment, and wisdom, worn proudly by someone who'd earned every mark, pound, and signs of age.

I slipped a pair of cool pajama bottoms over my nakedness, sleeping naked having become a habit when our youngest daughter had left for college. We were empty nesters, loving being in our house alone. I walked to the bathroom, hugging Zelda from behind, and as I nuzzled her neck, my singing joined hers, an impromptu duet. A beautiful way to greet the new day, singing, and making slow decadent love in a house devoid of people but full of love.

Afterwards, we talked about the events on the schedule for today as she showered and I shaved. I was torn two ways about everything on the agenda, happiness tinged with vestiges of sadness. Maybe the sadness would dissipate after breakfast. Zelda kissed me briefly, then put on her robe to go make breakfast. I took my shower, throwing on an old jogging suit, because it would be a no-frills kind of day. I walked downstairs to the kitchen where Zelda was making biscuit dough. It wouldn't be an easy breakfast this morning but a grand production. Our little kitchen radio was playing the blues, the volume low. Zelda making biscuits meant breakfast would be at least an hour to prepare.

"I'm going to step outside to the shed," I said. "I need to make sure everything is ready."

Zelda's face spoke volumes, a collage of emotions which only I would understand. Loss, hope, love, I read them all in her expression. I nodded my head, grateful that we understood each other without having to say painful, vulnerable things. Silence is a beautiful language.

As I made my way out of our house, the pictures on the walls greeted me. Wedding pictures, baptismal photos, graduation, trips, dinners, all reminders of the beautiful life we shared. Every sacrifice had been worth it. Today's sacrifice would be no different.

I almost whistled for Sparky to join me, nostalgia guiding my thoughts. Sparky was our Labrador who had been a fixture on mornings like this, a silent companion who understood the need for walks and space to think about life. When he died about three years ago, my heart cracked. I'd loved that damned dog so much that I never wanted another one. I didn't want to experience that type of loss again.

An old Chevy pickup truck and a brand-new minivan were parked in the driveway. The pickup had years on it and almost 400,000 miles. It was primarily my work vehicle now, no more road trips on the horizon. I'd only be driving to my job for another two years. Thirty years at the same job, having coworkers become almost like family, only to see them move on to another job or transcend into Eternity. Yeah, it was time to move on. I'd use the pickup today.

The minivan, a vehicle I'd laughed at other men for driving or owning, only had twelve miles on it. Zelda had picked it out yesterday, and I'd written a check on the spot, our days of car notes over forever. It's a wonderful feeling to arrive at a point in life where car notes and installment plans weren't necessary. No, we weren't rich by any means, but we were doing fine. The minivan was a sign of our new reality.

I unlocked the shed, flicking on the lights. I grabbed three fishing poles, sitting them by the door with my tacklebox. The shed held recreational stuff which made life more enjoyable. Except for the treadmill, which Zelda had bought on a whim, something about us living healthier lives. It had once resided in our bedroom, only to become a convenient hanger for clothes. Eventually, my son-in-law had helped me move it out here, unused, still serviceable, but not necessary. I made a mental note to put it for sale online.

In the middle of the shed was the covered thing which had occupied my thoughts. I pulled the covering off, revealing it slowly, my mind taking in every beautiful inch. The lights upon the chrome made it seem otherworldly, a visitor from another dimension. I folded the cover without even noticing, my eyes raking over this magnificent beast—a 1974 Harley Davidson Shovelhead Electra Glide. Purple was what caught the eye, then the chrome. A movie started playing in my mind, this motorcycle playing a starring role.

Thirty years ago, a young man still unsure of his life's course, met a witty, beautiful woman, and they took rides on his motorcycle, his purple Harley. Picnics, road trips, two kids in love with life and each other. Inevitably, they got married, and the kids became the parents of four children, and the road trips and roadside picnics went away. Baptisms, pageants, Little League, cotillions, proms, graduations, parties, family trips, college tuition, and all of the responsibilities of being parents made their idyllic times on the motorcycle seem like scenes from someone else's life.

Zelda and I would laugh, reminiscing about the fun we used to have. Her wearing short shorts, me proud that she was mine. I loved my kids and my life, but we clung to those memories, promising each other we'd go make new memories on the bike someday. Our helmets hung in the shed, mine purple with *Bruiser* written on it, hers lavender, reading simply *Z*.

Over the years, I'd maintained it, waiting for the day when we would be free to roam about again. When our youngest daughter left for college, we thought we would jump on our Harley and go on adventures.

Ten years ago, Zelda started her own business, and her time became almost non-existent for trips. When we went on vacations, the kids came, then later on, their spouses and the grandkids. The Harley just sat in the shed, with us maybe riding it once in a blue moon.

Recently, Zelda and I started talking about road trips again. There was a long moment of silence as we were forced to acknowledge we weren't those kids anymore. Life happens, and some things fall by the wayside, things you thought were cornerstones of your existence but were just things.

My grandsons played Little League, my granddaughter's in ballet and tap classes, and sometimes we were needed to ferry them around. We were grandparents, basking in the pleasures of this new reality.

The highways weren't as motorcycle friendly as they once were, and the nervousness associated with riding wasn't conducive to going on getaways with the bike.

I smelled her scent before she spoke. My Zelda, my partner

in this beautiful struggle known as life. She handed me a mug of coffee. We stood there, companionably silent, staring at the bike.

"Breakfast is ready," she said. "What time is the guy coming?"

"Around noon. He's putting it on a flatbed," I said. "His check cleared yesterday, so it's his now. I don't wanna be here for it. I'll leave the keys, and I'll grab the boys and take them fishing."

Zelda regarded my face, hers solemn as well. When I'd bought the bike all those years ago, I hadn't known that thirty-something years later it would be ten times more valuable. I wished we were still those kids, but we grew up.

Zelda's smile was a welcome sight, as if she had just had an epiphanic moment. "We're grandparents now, Bruiser. Our lifestyle has changed, as have our realities," she said. She kissed me then, reminding me that our spark was still there. "Keep the helmets though. Our days of riding on a motorcycle may be over, but we're still Bruiser and Zee. The adventures aren't over, merely shifting in a new direction."

I hugged her, thankful she was my partner, best friend, lover, and wife. Her whisper in my ear made my insides light up, hope renewed by her few simple words.

"Let's go buy a camper," she whispered.

The possibilities are endless ...

***

For more information on this author, visit:
marlonhayes.wixsite.com/author

KAWATKA
JON HEATH ⚡

8/10: My name is Zander, and I have finally found meaning in my work. Being an engineer has had its ups and downs, but after choosing to use my abilities to serve others rather than myself, I have realized my true purpose. The people of Kawatka, Africa deserve every advantage we can give them, and hopefully, I can help provide the fresh water their village desperately needs. In a country ripped apart by civil unrest, plague, and poverty, a little piece of mind can work wonders. In this case, a wonder will be what is expected of me. Accompanying me on this project is my friend Caitlyn—a linguist—and her husband Pete. Cait studied at Oxford like myself and graduated with honors in foreign studies. We met at a gathering of like-minded alumni, all with dreams of helping the less fortunate. Knowing just enough of the local language to get us by, she and Pete, who finished nursing school around the time this opportunity presented itself, decided to come with me.

It almost never rains here in northern Africa. Annually, this part of the world has the driest climate, making it very difficult to survive. There is fresh water deep underground that can be accessed with wells that can provide for every tribe and village around, but no one with the means to provide seems to care. I care. My drill design can be rotated into the ground manually by only four people, though I have never actually built it. The idea is to have two people push from one side of a vertically standing device with levers attached to the sides, while at the same time having two more simultaneously push from the other. After each ninety-degree rotation, the ratchet-style winch can easily be pulled back into position, allowing the four to push again. The drill itself is fashioned sturdily to the end of a log, which is riveted by hand into a helix pattern, allowing it to mesh with the mechanism to drive the drill into the earth a little with each rotation. Once the log is almost completely driven into the ground, we pour water into the hole and prep a second tree to be placed on top of the first, so the logs can be turned in unison. The only downfall to this design is the irony of having to use water to dig a well to get water. This can't be helped. I hope to have the well operational to the tribe before month end.

8/24: Preparations have been completed for the better part of a week, but we were forced to wait until today for the supply plane from the United Kingdom. These supply runs are a vital part of the survival of the tribe, so it was very difficult explaining to the Kawatkans that some of the water given to them so generously would need to be used not for cooking and drinking but for pouring down a hole. Luckily, we had Cait to explain this to them. A couple days after being presented with our plans, the Kawatkans finally decided to let us use water left over from the children's baths. Finally, we can get started.

8/28: It has been three days since we started drilling and sixty-one since the last rainfall. We grinded to a stop for the fifth time today, about sixty feet into the ground. Still no sign of water. I expected this. This will be our last two gallons; probably enough to get us another ten feet or so. Assessing the three logs we have in the hole, we pour one gallon and get started again. This is a very slow process. Luckily, after catching word from the council of what it is we are trying to accomplish, we've had our fair share of volunteers to help work the drill. You can tell there are eyes on us, however, wondering if we'll succeed.

9/19: It has been three weeks since we have run out of water. The drill has not functioned since then. We are approximately seventy-three feet down. I feel tension starting to build in the tribe as the locals are starting to doubt my ability to make the well work. As I walk through the village, I can feel them eyeing me, and it seems I'm not the hero they need me to be. I start to doubt myself as well, wondering if this whole thing will be for nothing. I keep telling myself that the next supply plane is coming.

10/1: The Kawatkans are asking Cait many questions. They seem to have in their heads that we're the ones controlling the supply planes. She seemed very troubled by the look on her face today. I tried to ask her what they said, but she just assured me everything was okay. I don't know if I believe her. There still hasn't been a hint of rain. How do these people live like this? Pete suggests that maybe I should try to force the drill into the ground without water. I believe this will just destroy it and our chances along with it. Maybe if it was made better ... But I did the best I could with what I had.

10/2: The supply plane came today, but we never saw any supplies. We swear we heard it overhead though. Cait thinks maybe they got intercepted by the local rebels. I hope this isn't the case. Pete is running out of meds for the village, and without water, more and more people are getting sick. The tribe is reaching a breaking point with us; I can see it in their eyes.

10/2 – Second Entry: Breaking point was an understatement. Today, I witnessed something unbearably hard to write about. The Kawatkans killed Cait, cut her up, and hung her upside down, draining her blood into whatever pottery they had lying around. She was not able to hold them off anymore. In other news ... the drill is functioning again. This will be my last entry. I can't take writing these events anymore.

***

For more information on this author, visit:
Baconb1t.blogspot.com

SUPERHERO FOR SALE
MARC HEMINGWAY

The intercom buzzed; the man behind the desk sighed. "Yes?"

"Mr. Black, your eleven o'clock is here."

Ten minutes early. He sighed once more. "Fine, show him in."

There was a light tap on the glass panel of the office door, which was followed instantly by the sound of a shattered window. The door handle turned, and a nervous—and quite sweaty—head appeared around the side of the door, followed by the rest of the body as a man edged into the room. Mr. Black noticed that the man was wearing a colourful homemade mask over his eyes. He also could see the edges of what looked to be a cape, made out of curtains.

"Take off the mask and have a seat," said Mr. Black, motioning towards the chair next to the desk.

"I can't," came the reply, "it's my, um, secret identity."

Sigh.

"No, your real identity is your secret identity, not … this." He gestured up and down the masked man's red, white, and blue attire.

"Oh, right. Didn't realise. I still can't take it off though, it'd go against my name."

"Let me guess … Masked Avenger, perhaps?"

"It was just an idea," said the man, looking embarrassed. Not wanting to make eye-contact, he suddenly found his boots extremely interesting.

"No," said Black. "Already taken."

"Oh, that's a shame. By who?"

"By the Masked Avenger."

"Right."

"Let's fill out your profile and go from there, shall we?" said Mr. Black as he pulled out a clipboard from a drawer in his desk. "Name?"

"Masked Aven— No, um, wait …"

"Start with your real name."

"Erm … Kevin."

"Alien or human?"

"Human."

"Superpowers?"

"Yes."

Sigh. "I mean, what superpowers do you have?"

"Oh, right, erm … I can run fast, like, as fast as a bullet, probably a bit faster if I were going downhill. I can fly a bit …"

"Can you leap buildings with a single bound?"

"Yes!"

"Are you super humanly strong?"

"Yes!"

"Not hearing anything new here, Kevin."

"Oh, what else … Erm … I can start fires really quickly."

"With your eyes?"

"No, with two sticks and dry leaves. I was in the scouts."

"Scouts, I see. Any other superpowers, something no one's ever heard of before?" Black found his mind wandering, wishing it was lunch time.

"I think that's it so far, to be honest."

"So how did they come about then? I'm guessing you haven't always had superpowers?"

Beneath his mask, Kevin's eyes widened. "I was bitten."

"By a spider?"

"By a mouse."

"A *radioactive* mouse?"

Kevin snorted. "Ha! No. A radioactive mouse, ha-ha! No! I

was at home messing about in the garage, I was supposed to be tidying up, but I was just looking through all the old boxes of junk we keep in there. I noticed in one box that a load of magazines had been chewed, so I emptied it out and found a nest." He stopped, looking lost in his thoughts.

"And then what did you do?"

"Well, I prodded it, didn't I! I heard a little noise, so I prodded again. That's when the thing bit me."

"It's then you realised you had your new powers, is it?"

"No, like I said, it's not because of the mouse. After I screamed, I mean, shouted out like a man, my mum came in, saw the blood, and took me to the hospital to get checked for rabies and stuff. When we were there, after a four-hour wait mind you, there was a power surge while they were giving me an X-ray."

"They gave you an X-ray to check for rabies from a mouse bite?"

"Yeah, they didn't want to, but my mum can be quite, umm … persistent. Better to be safe than sorry, she says. She also now says, 'Don't go prodding nests and getting bit again, you daft bugger.'"

"Was it your mum's idea to come here today?"

"Yeah," said Kevin. "She's heard about you, the celebrity agent that only looks after superheroes, so my mum, we, I decided to make an appointment." He pointed at Black, as though to make a point.

Black looked at his papers and once again sighed. "Do you have any idea of how many of you guys I get through here a day, Kevin? You're the eighth today, and it's not yet lunch."

"I just want to help. Apart from getting loads of sponsorship deals and stuff so my mum doesn't need to work."

"That's the thing, Kevin; there are too many superheroes at the moment and not enough peril, not enough trouble to go around."

"But—" Kevin began.

"I'm sorry; my books are overflowing as it is. Try again next year."

"I see," Kevin replied. "My mum's not going to be happy about this. Thanks for your time though."

As Kevin turned to the door, Black spoke. "Unless …"

"Yes?" Kevin looked over his shoulder.

"Ah, never mind."

"Go on! Please?" He turned fully towards the desk, interest fully piqued.

"Well … my 'other' book is quite empty."

Kevin's forehead wrinkled. "Your 'other' book?"

"For the 'other' side. You see, with superheroes coming out of the woodwork—"

"Like Captain Woodworm?"

"I didn't … Not as literal, Kevin. With superheroes being ten a penny, there are quite a few openings for, well, supervillains."

"Oh. Oh! I'm not sure my mum would like it. What's the pay like?"

"All you can get your hands on and more. I'm sure your mum will see that you're helping to keep the heroes in work, wouldn't she?"

Kevin looked thoughtful. "Prospects?"

Black leaned over his desk and spoke the next two words slowly. "World. Domination."

"That'd make my mum proud! I guess I'm in! Where do I sign?"

"Leave your details with my secretary on your way out, and I'll be in touch."

"Thanks, Mr. Black! You won't regret this!" Kevin shot out of the office in a blur of colour and curtain fabrics.

Black pushed back in his chair and picked up the phone. He

waited for the answer on the other end, then said just five words.
"Fang? It's Black. Got another."

Click

Black hated this part of the job, but at least it paid well, and that's what makes the world go round.

That didn't make him a bad person, did it?

Maybe a bit, but the pay was worth it.

The intercom buzzed.

RUBIES
LARA HENERSON

It all began when my fingernails ran away. It was 11:54 on a Thursday night, and I was buried deep in a work project that was due in just a few hours. I sat at my desk in an old gray t-shirt and checkered pajama bottoms, bathed in the flickering fluorescence of my desktop monitor, hands clacking away on the keyboard. My eyes were glued so tightly to the screen that everything that surrounded it was a mere blur, swimming out of focus in the periphery.

As I was entering the updated figures into column *D* of the spreadsheet, I felt a subtle, dull prying. I ignored it. I'd been sitting here, working for eight hours already. The aches and pains of the nine-to-five life were one thing, but when you did as much overtime as I did, you had to tune these things out, even when your body was crying out to you, begging to be stretched.

But the prying sensation persisted, and after a few minutes, I finally conceded and yanked my eyes from the spreadsheet, annoyed.

Perhaps it was a rebellion, or perhaps they merely wished to inconvenience me, to add one more small tile to the mosaic of my stress, but as I looked down at my hands, I discovered that one by one the nails of my right hand—painted burgundy and slightly chipped—were shimmying themselves off my fingers. They scuttled in a line across the keyboard, from key to key, like ants across the floor. It began with my right hand; I suppose because I'm right-handed. Almost immediately though, my left fingernails followed suit. Their path veered off to the right and then onto the scratched pine of the desk, the ten of them arranged from largest to smallest, a procession that snaked its way into my desk drawer, which was cracked open.

I let out an exasperated breath. *Of all times for something like this to happen ...* I was busy. I had things to deal with, and my hope was to squeeze in at least an hour of sleep. I just didn't have time for this. I looked down at the naked ends of the tops of my fingers—smooth and pink and virginal. My focus, so intense only a moment ago, was suddenly waning. *Thanks a lot, fingernails.* Without a second thought, I reached for the desk drawer with the intention of retrieving them.

No sooner had I grasped the knob though, then my hand came away sticky. It was coated in a thick, creamy, pale-green substance. I put my hand to my lips. Mint frosting, probably homemade. I narrowed my eyes. *What is this? Some kind of conspiracy? Some force hell bent on keeping me from finishing my work and going to bed?* I adjusted the desk lamp, glaring at the cupcake that now replaced the knob of the drawer. I'd mashed it, slightly. Vengeance in my heart, I plucked the distracting treat off the drawer and shoved it into my mouth. It was mildly stale. It occurred to me that I hadn't had dinner. Or lunch. Or breakfast.

But I was getting distracted. These numbers weren't going to input themselves, and I had ninety-eight more rows and sixty more columns to go. I wiped my nail-less fingers on the leg of my pajama pants, adjusted my hair into a hasty ponytail, and turned my attention back to the monitor.

The spreadsheet was gone. Instead, I was looking through the monitor at the view that usually stretched beyond the bay windows just behind me. There was the dark lawn, the amber pool of light from the streetlamp, and across the street, an identical house in which the kindergarten teacher was changing into her nighty from behind thin gauzy curtains. I blinked, swiveled in my chair to look out the bay window where the view should be. And that's where my spreadsheet was. Framed by cream-painted wood, endless columns and rows were projected, made up of millions of tiny pixels, the curser in column *D*, row 27, still blinking persistently at me to continue. I scratched my head, looked back at the monitor. The kindergarten teacher had turned off her bedroom light. *Bitch*, I thought, jealous beyond reason that this near stranger was going to bed while I was still stuck here at my desk. I watched as twin headlights traveling down the street passed our mailbox, behind the "trash" folder that hovered over it.

I had to keep working. I took the keyboard onto my lap and turned myself towards the window. I had to readjust myself a little in order to still reach for the mouse. I rolled it across the desk and clicked, but as I did so, it bit me. I yelped, more out of surprise than pain, and pulled my hand away. The furry thing scuttled off behind the file cabinet. *Typical*, I thought, sucking the wound on my hand where the mouse's teeth had punctured the skin. I choked, spat out something hard.

It was a little red bead. A ruby, I realized, rolling it in the palm of my hand. For the first time that night, I shifted my focus away from my work. *This*, I thought, *is extraordinary*. I set it aside on the mouse pad, watching it glow faintly like a tiny ember. I felt suddenly proud that I'd produced the gem all by myself. Maybe I'd have it set into a pendant.

I contemplated the puncture of the side of my hand just beneath my naked pinkie. Surely, there was more where that came from. I looked to the mason jar beside my monitor, pulled out a letter opener from among the pens and pencils. It was a little dull, but with a bit of sawing, I thought I could access more rubies. My heart thumped with excitement as I set the dull blade against my wrist and began dragging it against my skin. It didn't hurt, only tickled. Like being licked by some rough-tongued kitten.

Soon, more rubies were spilling out of my skin, perfectly spherical, lustrous. I gazed at them, filled with lust, and greed, and more lust. I moaned as they tumbled into the keyboard on my lap, rolling off and clattering to the floor, muffled by the beige Ikea area rug. I was the creator, endlessly fruitful, a bottomless mine. I had a purpose. And the rubies, they were so beautiful I just couldn't stop. I switched over to my left wrist, eager to produce more and more rubies. I was obsessed with them, wanted to roll in them, scoop them up into my hands and let them cascade onto the floor in a torrent. I thought of the gorgeous necklaces I could make, with earrings to match, the bracelets and anklets. About how I could sell them all, never work again ...

It was several hours before my husband came into my office, wondering why I'd never come to bed. When he opened the door, the little crimson beads poured over him like a tidal wave, rolling out onto the hardwood floor of the hallway. He waded through them, panic on his face, the soles of his slippers crunching over my precious rubies as he propelled himself towards my desk chair. By then, my skin was empty, draped over the back of my chair like a coat. Meanwhile, I had become the walls.

I watched him, my poor husband. He screamed, his voice suddenly morphing into the percussive notes of an oboe, perfectly in tune, which was surprising because my husband had never had much musical talent. I watched from my wallpapered expanse, pitying him. But I couldn't help it, after all. I hadn't asked my fingernails to run away, or for the drawer knob to morph into a cupcake, or for the monitor and the window to swap views, or for the computer mouse to come alive. I hadn't even asked for the rubies—those beautiful gems rolling every which way, a beautiful sea of crimson flooding the floor.

I wanted to reach out, to hug my husband, to embrace him from all sides. The oboe notes continued to spill from his throat, high and clear, as I closed in on him, my smooth walls coming closer and closer until I touched the white fabric of his t-shirt and the dark hairs of his bare arms. I squeezed further, trying to show this man, whom I loved, that he was not alone, that I was still here. As I compressed him, more rubies poured out from his nose, from his eye sockets, shot out of his mouth like hundreds, no, thousands of tiny red bullets. They were breathtaking—a deeper, darker shade than mine.

Soon, he was flattened, paper thin, and my heart was full of oboe notes, of rubies, and of the beautiful jewelry we could make together.

SAXY JAZZ
KARI HOLLOWAY

Harley stirred her drink, and the little red straw disappeared into the colorful cocktail. She didn't know why she'd ordered it. Three days a week, she'd come sit at this bar after work, sit in the same chair, and order the same drink, only because it was a blip of color in a rather monochrome selection of wine coolers and beers. But she never drank it.

The first time she came was a fluke. A flat tire forced her to pull over on her way back from a wedding. With her phone dead and her charger AWOL, she had no choice but to look for a phone. With nothing else opened, she'd stumbled inside from the rain. She expected to find past-their-prime players doing covers of songs. What she found instead was a man who made her soul vibrate.

Harley caught herself whispering the words of "Ain't No Sunshine." She straightened her shirt, wondering why she hadn't stopped at home and changed from her work attire. Her messy bun with the pencil stuck in it wasn't sexy, just sad.

"You gonna actually drink it this time?" John, the bartender, asked. He laid her change next to her napkin. "I can get you a water or a cola."

"Oh." Her lips formed a perfect O. The thought had never crossed her mind. "Water, please." She tugged a bill from the pile, but John shook his head.

"On the house." He dug around the cooler and pulled out a damp water bottle. After he ran a cloth over it, he set it beside her drink.

"Thanks," she mouthed before turning around on the stool.

It didn't matter Harley had never heard the man's voice. The notes coming from his sax were warm and tempting, inviting her in like a fire on winter's day.

"Last round." John gave the call, but he was only doing it for show—she was the only patron.

She rubbed her hands against her pants. Slowly exhaling, she tried to ease the butterflies trying to force her ribcage apart. Leaving her change on the bar, she slid from the barstool. She weaved between tables, focused on the glint of lights dancing across the saxophone. Her knee brushed against a chair, sending it scraping against the floor, and she paused. Through squinted eyes, she risked a glance at him.

He stood on stage, holding a cloth. He didn't say anything, but the look in his eyes was pure curiosity. He ran a hand along his pulled-back hair and smoothed an invisible wrinkle in his solid-colored shirt.

She was enchanted with him as her eyes followed the path of his hand over his dark jeans still sporting a crisp crease. "I'm Harley."

"Friends call me Pipes." He tossed the rag into the saxophone case and offered his hand.

"Pipes. Is that because you play like an angel?" She smirked as she shook his hand.

"An angel, huh? Never been called that." He smirked. He tucked his hands into his pockets and shifted his weight. "They call me Pipes because I've always wanted a Harley. I've been saving up for one." He rubbed the back of his neck, and a slow blush crept up his neck.

"Well, Pipes." Harley leaned over, wrapped her hand in his shirt, and pulled him close. "How about you and your sax take me for a ride?" She kissed him on his cheek to hide the crimson blush coloring her cheeks "Maybe we'll get to be something more than two people who enjoy jazz."

***

For more information on this author, visit: kariholloway.com

THEY COME
WHIMSY GARDENER ⚡

Just the thought of what lie ahead for me was almost too much to bear. I knew this day would come; I had tried to prepare for it. But, one can only prepare so much.

"Make sure to be well rested," I was informed, but how can one sleep knowing—or I should say, *not* knowing—what was in store for them? After much tossing and turning for what seemed to be hours, I was finally able to get some sleep. When dawn finally arrived, I awoke with dread at facing the day. I ate what I could keep down and went on my way.

After arriving and entering my station, I tried to stay focused on what I was required to do. As I made my rounds, making sure we were well stocked, I could feel my hands begin to tremble, and a nervous chill swept across my flesh. I swallowed hard as I attempted to push away a fear that was slowly working its way over my nerves. I rubbed my sweaty palms on the front of my pants and took a few deep breaths trying to remain calm.

I passed by one in my group who was busy making sure their area was ready; they stopped to look my way long enough for us to give each other knowing nods before we went about our own business of preparing. I made my way back and swallowed again, a lump starting to form in the back of my throat. I looked around wide-eyed and faked a small smile in hopes to ease the worried lines between my brows.

Those who were in charge were moving across the floor very quickly, scribbling things down on their notepads they carried, and mumbling to themselves. Every once in a while, one would stop by my station to ask me questions. Satisfied with my answers, they would move along. I could sense a mild panic in their lightly raised voices.

From where I stood at my station, I could see outside. I watched as the sky that had known darkness only hours before begun to show the first faint signs of light. I ran a shaking hand through my hair and began to pace the floor. Fear arose in me as time ticked on. Back and forth I walked, taking slow, deep breaths. I glanced up at the sounds of yelling and fast talking as something was forgotten and had to quickly be remedied before it was too late.

Panic began at the base of my spine and slowly worked its way up to my shoulders, causing discomfort. I rolled each of them, then my head, hearing a few pops of the joints while I tried to relieve the pressure of built-up tension. I took a few more deep breaths, feeling the air fill my lungs, releasing it slowly through my dry, parched lips. I picked up my water bottle with shaking fingers, undid the cap, and took a few slow sips. As the cool water flowed down my throat, I thought back to a time before this, a time back before I had to worry about such a day.

My thoughts were brought back to the present when I heard a loud crash. I jumped, spilling my water down the front of my shirt, and I spun around quickly. I couldn't make out what had made the noise, but all the yelling that followed told me it was not that far from where I stood. I swallowed again, running my trembling hand over the front of my shirt. The coolness of the water that penetrated the fabric felt good against the heat of my flushed skin.

I began having this sickening, queasy, nauseous feeling in my cheeks as panicking thoughts ran through my head. How much longer till all hell breaks loose? *I can't do this!* I thought. *I can't go through with this! I've got to get out of here! I need to leave, now! No! No!* I argued with myself. *I promised to be here and to help.* In fact, I had no other choice. I was told that I had to be here. That it was my ... job ... to help out. I only have to hang in there, be strong, I tried to convince myself. *I can do this, I can, and I ... must, no matter what happens.* But, how can I? How can I stay when every cell in my body was screaming out the same word: run? Leave, leave now, and just go! What's the worst that could happen?

As my feet refused to leave my area, I knew the answer to that. I knew I had no choice but to stay and face the unknown. Besides, I thought, looking around me, it's not like I would be alone in this. I'd be surrounded by those more experienced than I. Those who have fought the good fight and survived. I coughed, running my fingers through my hair once again, feeling a light perspiration forming at my temples.

It was at this moment that I glanced outside and gasped. Sheer panic took over, and I froze in my spot, unable to move, barely able to breathe. "No, no! Is it happening already? Is this when my life, as I know it, ends?" I stood ready, barely prepared, as my breath became more rapid—in and out in short quick spurts. Feeling lightheaded, my thoughts swirled and tangled in my mind. The buzz around me was slowly drowned out by the ascended pounding of my own heart in my ears. I subconsciously ran my hands together; they felt cold and clammy, and my chest felt hot and tight.

As if in slow motion, I watched outside while they approached. These beings, whose eyes were focused intently on their own mission, made their way closer and closer. I swallowed back the cereal I had forced down my throat for breakfast just hours ago as I fought back tears. I didn't want anyone around me to think I was weak, but the truth was, I was scared to death.

Although I was shaking with trepidation, I readied myself as more and more arrived. I glanced around me and noticed I wasn't the only one who looked like they would rather be somewhere else. And yet, seemed to be those whom appeared to be confident—either they truly were, or they hid their own inadequacies very well.

My thoughts were interrupted with shrieks, yelling, and earthshaking pounding of feet. I turned my head just in time to witness what appeared to be a stampede of mindless bodies trampling over each other to win some crazed unknown race. I pleaded with my body to move, to do something, anything, but frozen in place, I was held, as if by some unknown force. I remained at my assigned station. This is it, I thought, this is my day of reckoning. I stayed steadfast as my thoughts returned to just the night before; I had enjoyed what was possibly my last meal, surrounded by my family and friends. *Would I ever see them again? I* questioned myself.

The day was nothing short of pure terror. Hour after long agonizing hour passed as I did what I had to do to survive. Never before had I seen such intense frenzy. Although I had heard the horror stories, nothing could have prepared me for this. As the day of total and complete chaos for me came to an end, I returned home exhausted but thankful that it was over, at least for now. And as I hung up my apron with the shiny badge with my name on it and flung myself on to the bed and stared up at the ceiling, I was finally able to release a long sigh of relief. I was ever so grateful that Black Friday came around only once a year.

THERE'S NO SUNSHINE IN HELL
LAURIE GARDINER

I've been stuck in this hellhole alone for three days. The little bit of food Johnny left on my bedside table is gone, and a week-old broken hip has me bedridden and unable to get to the kitchen. Heavy curtains banish light from this ten-by-twelve cell, and it's been weeks since I've seen daylight. I crave the warmth of the sun on my face.

My nostrils burn with the pungent smell of stale urine. The heap of used adult diapers beside the bed grows bigger each day. Thank God he left the package within my reach, but only a few are left.

The tall, plastic cup on the nightstand taunts me, and my tongue darts across cracked lips. I scoot my body higher in the bed and reach for the cup. My hand shakes and drops to the pillow. Frustration sticks in my parched throat like a bitter, undissolved pill.

Johnny's never been gone this long before. He's never left me without food for more than a day. Something's wrong. I feel it deep in my gut. Or maybe that's the hunger pains that stab at my insides like tiny sharp needles each time my stomach rumbles.

The pain does serve a purpose; it tells me I'm alive. And despite the hunger and the thirst, I needed a reprieve. My battered body became the scapegoat for my son's uncontrollable anger.

Maybe he's in jail. He probably got drunk and ended up in a fight or tried to drive home and got pulled over. Or was in an accident.

My heart thumps against my ribs at the thought. What if he's dead? What will happen to me?

I glance at the cup. If I ration, allow myself only a few sips a day, there might be enough water to last two or three days. Then what? I'll lie here in my own filth and die of thirst, that's what.

Better to dump the water. Without it, I'll likely be dead in a couple days. Death by dehydration would be quicker and much kinder than the slow, sadistic method old age and emphysema prefer.

Despite knowing they've led to my demise, I still crave a cigarette. The thought of smoking sends my lungs into spasms. I cough and heave, my body curling inward as the pain rips through my chest. When the bout ends, my head flops onto the pillow. Air wheezes reluctantly in and out of my damaged lungs as I struggle to breathe.

I should have oxygen. The doctor told me months ago that I need it. But Johnny says we can't afford it. Between my pension and the money in my account, there should be enough, but I made the stupid mistake of giving Johnny my bankcard and PIN when he came home, proclaiming he got clean. No doubt that was a lie and he's spent it all on drugs and booze and gambling and women.

I don't dare complain though. Complaining only makes him mad, and he's nasty when he's mad, just like his old man.

My tongue feels like sawdust in my mouth. I lean to one side, reaching for the cup. As my fingers grasp the rim, pain radiates from my hip and shoots down my leg. I scream. My hand spasms and sends the cup bouncing to the floor.

With teeth clenched, I slump against the pillow and breathe deeply to calm the pain. The steady *drip drip drip* of water hitting the floor taunts me as I watch my life trickle from the edge of the table.

The realization that my time has come brings a strange sense of relief. With a sigh, I close my eyes and welcome the oblivion sleep brings.

The sound of a door closing wakes me. I have no idea how long I've slept, but the room is black. My heart beats faster when I hear the distinct shuffle of Johnny's uneven gait in the hallway. He stops outside my door, and I hold my breath. When he sees how badly off I am, he'll regret leaving me. He'll help me. He must; I'm his mother.

The bedroom door creaks open slowly, and he stands silhouetted against the faint light behind him, his head nearly touching the doorframe. He ducks into the room and flicks on the overhead light.

I cry out and squeeze my eyes shut against the sudden brightness.

"It stinks in here."

I open one eye half way.

He's looming over the bed and sneering at me, his upper lip curled in disgust.

When I try to speak, it comes out as a croak. I wet my lips with my tongue and whisper, "Water."

He slowly shakes his head and leans over me until our faces are inches apart. The smell of stale cigarette smoke and sweet rum wafts over me.

"I thought you'd be dead by now," he says.

My eyes blink in surprise. "What do you mean?"

Without a word, he opens the closet door, drops to his knees, and begins removing things.

"Johnny? What're you doing?"

He empties the closet, stacking boxes against the wall and tossing clothes and shoes into a pile.

"I was six years old when Pop left—old enough to know what was happening, but not to understand why. I blamed myself, thinking if I'd behaved better, maybe he would've stayed. You blamed me too."

"I did not—"

"You did! I know you did. You told me over and over every time you got drunk." He sends things flying into the room behind him with a ferocity that leaves me cringing. His voice becomes a high falsetto as he attempts to mimic me. "'It's your fault, Johnny. He wouldn't have left if it weren't for you. He never wanted a kid in the first place.'"

The closet is empty. Johnny climbs to his feet and approaches me, kicking urine-logged diapers out of his way.

"I spent the next ten years hoping you were wrong, waiting for him to walk through the door. By the time I realized he wasn't coming back, I didn't care anymore—not about him, not about you, not about anyone or anything."

He stops at my bedside, slides his massive, meaty hands beneath my body, and lifts me into his arms.

Pain streaks through my hip, causing me to moan. "Please don't."

He carries me to the closet. My breath comes in short gasps. I try to struggle, but it's no use; I'm so weak I can barely move. He kneels, places me on the closet floor, and sits back on his heels.

"Why?" I ask.

I know why, but I want him to look me in the eyes and tell me.

He stares over my head as he speaks. "Do you remember what you did to me? When the drinking got real bad, you'd lock me in my bedroom closet so you could go out partying, shooting up, hooking—whatever else you did."

There's no point defending myself. I've done all those things and more. Guilty as charged. No excuses.

"The first few times, it was only for a few hours, but then you started staying away longer. You left me alone for days in that dark closet. I had to piss in the corner. My hands and feet were bloody and raw from trying to open the door. There were times when I didn't see sunlight for days."

His fists curl into balls and he finally looks at me, his dark eyes boring into mine. They are so full of hate it causes a shudder to course through my body. Even so, I can't look away.

"I was just a little boy."

His body sways. He sits down hard, wraps his arms around his knees, and rocks back and forth as tears course down his cheeks.

My hand twitches with the urge to wipe them away, but I don't. It's too late now to be a mother.

"If you couldn't take care of me, why didn't you just give me away?"

"I'm sorry." It sounds pathetic even to my ears.

Johnny climbs onto his hands and knees and leans over me. "It's too late to be sorry, Ma. I want you to know what it felt like for me. You're going to die here, alone, in the dark, and then you're going straight to Hell."

He stands and closes the door.

The lock clicks as darkness envelopes me.

He's wrong about one thing. My Hell will end in this closet.

***

For more information on this author, visit: lauriegardiner.me

TAKIN' PICTURES
SUSAN GIBBONS

Agnes laid in bed listening to the rain pound on the roof. Through her eyelids, she saw flashes of light that came in from her window. She counted down from ten until she heard the rumble of thunder.

"That's a four," she muttered. Agnes missed sitting on the porch with Stanley, her husband of sixty-three years, during storms. They would gently rock back and forth on their swing. "Angels are bowling."

She swore her husband responded, "God's takin' pictures." She remembered how Stanley sat up straight and smiled at the sky. When the lightning flashed again, he relaxed back into the swing. Agnes would lean her head against his shoulder while he patted her knee and continued to say, "Come on, Agnes. Let God get a picture of us together so, when we die, he knows to bring us back together." Agnes hated the thought of either of them dying as much as getting her picture taken.

Four years ago, it happened. Agnes was in the kitchen cooking breakfast while Stanley read the morning paper in his armchair. She called him in to eat. After a few minutes with Stanley not appearing in his seat at the table, she went in and found him. He was slumped over the side of his chair with the newspaper still opened on his lap. He died of a heart attack.

Agnes flung open her eyes. "Stanley! I'll meet you on the porch!" she called out. She raised the head of her bed and grabbed the rail to steady herself as she stood. Agnes shuffled across the floor to shut the door to her room. She scooted the rocking chair around to face the window. Thunder rattled the panes. She counted, then whispered, "Seven. Angels are bowling."

She blinked at the emptiness beside her. A tear escaped her eye as she whimpered, "Don't you wish you had cheered on the angels when you were alive?" She felt a hand pat her knee. She closed her eyes. The familiar scent of English Leather tickled her nose. "I miss you, Stanley. I keep thinking about you. The residents tell me I have restless-soul syndrome. I'll be with you soon."

"God's takin' pictures. Come on, Agnes." She heard Stanley breathe.

Agnes opened her eyes, looking up into the night sky. She smoothed down her hair, sat up as straight as she could with a smile, and waited for the next flash of light.

Her door creaked open, and someone hustled over toward her. "Mrs. Clevenger? What are you doing out of bed at this late hour?"

"I'm getting my picture taken."

***

For more information on this author, visit:
facebook.com/authorsusangibbons

LEAVING HOME
HANNAH GRIECO

Rena was thirsty and tired. Her legs and arms were coated in a thick, gray dust that wouldn't brush off. She used her left pointer finger to trace her name into her right forearm, next to the fading heart Grandpa had sketched earlier. The heart was already half full of dust again. She traced it, digging it back out.

"Rena." His voice was dry and cracked. "Rena can you see what color the flag is?"

She searched the horizon and saw a tiny flag far ahead. Just a blur, barely noticeable above the dead forest.

"Maybe black or brown? It's far away still."

Grandpa's eyes were closed. She wondered if he had eaten today. He was always pretending to eat, saving his protein mix in his pockets to give her as a snack later. He swayed for a moment, then righted himself.

"Grandpa, let's rest."

He didn't answer.

"I'm so tired. I'm going to sit down," she said.

She took his wrinkly, old-man hand, so soft and weak compared to hers, and guided him toward the side of the road. She put both of his hands on her shoulders to help him ease down to the ground. He was staring at the dirt as she searched through the thin cloth sack.

"I'm sorry," he whispered.

"Let's have a sip," she whispered back.

His head rose. He reached out to stop her, but it was too late. She had removed the cap and taken the smallest taste. Her eyes stung, like she might cry, but it had been a long time since she had felt tears on her cheeks.

"Drink a little, Grandpa. I can't walk there alone. Please drink."

Grandpa took the canteen and wet his lips, then handed it back to her. He reached into his pocket and pulled out a dirty plastic bag. The gripper had been lost long ago, and the top was torn badly.

"Let's share this," he said in a stronger voice. "Then we will walk to the flag."

They quickly finished the protein mix, despite their dry mouths. Despite their swollen throats. They ate, then they rose and began walking once more. Behind them, drawing closer, were the two women they had seen last night.

Also heading to the check-in station. Also waiting for the green flag.

"We must hurry." Grandpa moved more purposefully now.

Rena trotted to catch up with him, relieved that he seemed like himself again. He had been shrinking over the past week. Ever since they gave Rosa to the doctor and her husband.

The doctor had been clean and pretty. She'd explained that they would be picked up shortly for transport. That they had water and food. Grandpa had begged them to take Rena too. But the woman refused. She didn't want a big, dirty girl. She wanted a sweet baby. Her husband stood behind her, his face expressionless.

In the end, Rena and Grandpa watched them carry her little sister back to their living pod. The door slid closed behind the three of them, and the armed guards stepped back into place. There was no time to be say goodbye or be sad. They had to go.

Now they walked for a long time without speaking. Rena occasionally looked over her shoulder to see if the couple was gaining ground, and her grandfather would nudge her and mutter about focusing on the road. She could see the flag up ahead now. Definitely not green. A tattered black.

They weren't too late. They could still get there in time.

But it was getting dark by the time they could hear the noise of other people. It wasn't safe to just keep walking on the road. Grandpa craned his neck to get a better look in the dim evening light, but the flag was hidden in the gloom. There was no sunset, like usual. The haze was always too heavy at this time of day.

"We can walk behind those trees over there. We'll be okay if we're quiet." Grandpa immediately turned to leave the path.

"But you'll fall!" Rena argued. "We should wait until morning."

"The flag will change any time now."

He stepped into the forest, past the first band of dead trees, and continued on until she couldn't see him at all. Panicked, she ran after him. Then together they slowly crunched their way through twigs and brown moss, climbing over fallen trunks, scratching their limbs on thorns and sharp branches. They kept their hands out ahead of them, seeing with their fingertips as it got darker and darker.

They walked for hours. Grandpa was like a robot, never stopping or even slowing down. Not looking back at her until they were suddenly hit by an enormous roar from up ahead. His eyes lit up, and he grabbed Rena's arm.

"Come now. Quickly."

He pulled her back out to the road, where a bright spotlight was shining on a mass of shouting people. These were sleepwalkers with voices, zombies from an old-fashioned Hollywood movie ... but somehow still alive. Still wanting things. Their hands raised up to the tower where the light came from. Their screams blending together into a wall of sound.

Grandpa pushed her ahead of him now. Into the packed crowd. Somehow, he had the strength of ten young men, and she had a momentary memory of her father. His strong arms carrying her upstairs, his beard scratchy against her cheek. Then it was gone. Her grandfather had somehow moved them up to the metal gate, where a thin, balding man in a suit was surrounded by soldiers.

"She is only seven. She has many years ahead of her. Save her, please!"

Rena realized with horror what was happening, and she tried to turn back to him. "No! Grandpa, no!" But he shoved her forward, away from him.

The gate opened, the guards pulling her inside before slamming it shut again. The crowd behind her swelled furiously and swallowed her grandfather whole.

***

For more information on this author, visit:
www.hannahgrieco.com

FIRST THANKSGIVING
SARAH KAMINSKI ⚡

Seven months, two weeks, three days—hours, minutes, seconds are the spare change of time. We left the courtroom, still giddy from our spontaneity, and gobbled cupcakes at the store around the corner.

"My mother will love you," he promised.

I wasn't so sure.

Seven months, two weeks, and three days passed by us so quickly, those early months full of newlywed bliss, broken only by the necessary arguments over newly shared space.

"You got married too quickly," my mother scolded.

"We were together for three months," I reminded her. "Longer than you and Dad."

"We were older."

This is true, but when you're in love, there's nothing else to do.

Now, I stood in the corner of the kitchen and watched my mother-in-law prepare a meal, arguably the most important meal of the year. She applied a healthy coat of cooking spray to the interior of a blue and yellow Crock-Pot. Twenty seconds she sprayed; I counted with eyebrows raised in alarm.

"Can I help you?"

"Oh, no, no, no!" She bustled across the kitchen and dumped boiled potatoes into the ceramic dish and began mashing with enthusiasm. "I've got it. You just sit, relax."

A toddler, one of my new nieces, grabbed at my skirt, fingers already sticky with sweets.

"Play phone?" she whispered, fast and soft, how small children do, nearly inaudible. Words mumbled together only parents can translate.

"What?"

"Play phone!" she repeated, pointing at my hand.

I shook my head, imagining the afternoon spent cleaning syrup and grease off of the screen. "No."

She began to cry. I looked to my mother-in-law for help, but she only frowned at me.

"Here, darling," she said, handing over her own phone and a sugar cookie with whipped red icing.

The girl stuffed it into her mouth and grinned, darting off, her pain forgotten.

His mother looked back at me. "Children are sticky."

"I didn't want her to break my phone."

"Maybe you shouldn't have children, if you can't handle them."

Had he spoken to her about our arguments? Had he called her to vent frustration that I wanted to wait?

I nodded. "I'll go sit in the other room."

I wandered the rooms filled with new relatives, strangers I must now call family. Women compared clothes and shopped for shoes on their phones; men played poker, drank beers, and shouted at the football game on TV. Children raced through the rooms, unsupervised, hitting each other, stepping on toes, and toppling empty drinks. Through it all, me on the outside, watching, wondering where I might fit in. Wondering why he had married me at all. I watched the clock on the wall, seconds ticked by with painfully slow rhythm.

"Dinner is ready!"

All heads turned to look toward the kitchen where his mother stood proudly with arms wide. "Fix a plate!"

At once the room shifted, feet met the floor, footsteps pounded. People crowded the kitchen table, loading industrial-sized paper plates with food and plastic cutlery, grabbing paper napkins with turkeys on them. They returned to their seats in the living room in less than a minute, eyes glued to the TV as they shoveled food into their mouths.

"Go on, dear," my new mother-in-law said, gesturing to the table and smiling.

"I'm allergic to garlic."

"Oh?" Another frown.

"I thought he told you?"

"No."

"I'm sorry."

She frowned and pointed out dishes. "Avoid this, and this, and this."

I dished a plate, small portions of all that remained: canned cranberry sauce, still ridged on the sides, a dinner roll, raw vegetables from a tray, gelatinous yams that swam in congealed butter, and broccoli dripping in cheese. "Thank you."

I stood on the edges of the room until my husband called to me. "Sit down!"

I tasted the broccoli first—too salty and cold; I pushed the rest aside. The yams were greasy and undercooked. I watched the room as everyone, even children, swallowed barely chewed bites without looking up, each in his own little world, consuming without tasting. I bit into a carrot.

"You're not hungry?" She stood over me, watching every move.

"I'm feeling a bit queasy."

"Hmm." A third frown, eyebrows knit, and she walked away.

Hours passed, the football game wound to a close. "Those fucking Patriots!" someone snarled. I blinked. *What a thing to say on a national holiday.* In the basement, a child started screaming in pain, but no one moved to investigate. Twenty seconds later, the child emerged with tears staining her cheeks to be coddled and doted on by her mother.

An hour passed, then another. Pies bought at Tippin's the day before were passed around. We gathered our coats, thick grey wool and buttoned carefully. I stepped gratefully into the cool November air, thankful to be out of the crowded house, the warmth from the oven, the press of so many bodies crammed into such a small space. My stomach growled.

I paused and turned back as his mother grabbed his arm.

"I just hate your wife!"

"I know," he said calmly. "I'm sorry."

***

For more information on this author, visit:
sarahkaminskiauthor.com

RECOLLECTED: SANGUINE
PYRA KANE ⚡

Everything was fine until the cracks grew bigger. The rumbling is what pulled my attention from memory 508, a comic book of supernatural deaths. With a noise like glass breaking, the hair-thin lines that'd appeared in the surrounding void a few months ago split like the fractures in my skulls. Spider-web fissures covered the ground, the rounded walls, up to the ceiling's center. An orange light—the good side of my Person's mind—forced its way through, turning my lovely black abyss into a holy shithole.

My heart constricted as I looked to the screen embedded in the opposite wall. What'd been a nice view of my Person's kitchen was now static. Unless my Person had their eyes inches from a faulty TV channel, something was up.

Rising to my feet, I tossed memory 508 aside and made my way to the screen, stepping over my skull collection and fragments of times long past. The glass was cool to the touch, unchanging under my fingertips. I pursed my lips and rapped my knuckles against the screen. An image flickered before the static resumed. My blood ran cold. Through their eyes, I saw a vast expanse of tile spread from under my Person's cheek. Their arm lay motionless on the floor, and underneath their fingers was a small white bottle labeled, *Tylenol.*

My legs went weak, and I stumbled back, nearly tripping on a cranium. Was this really happening? My Person couldn't have hit their limit this soon, could they? That question was answered when shards of the void fell past my nose. They clattered against the floor before falling into the fissures, engulfed in orange.

I fell to my knees and put one eye to the fissure, peering in. The room below was like mine but reminiscent of a tangerine and full of stuffed animals and happy things. There was a figure identical to myself, except they didn't have the stitches at the corners of their mouth extending out as an artificial smile, nor was their body missing chunks of flesh. They were crouched in the room's center, hugging their stomach like they were about to hurl. Of course our Person's most-used personality half would feel the effects of their actions.

I cupped a hand around my mouth and called out, "How bad is it?"

Their only answer was a chorus of pained and sickly moaning.

I scratched my head, then nearly lost my balance to a tremor. The fissures expanded and spread to the lower room, looking as if they were trying to peel that tangerine. The Good Personality Half fell flat on their back, staring up at me with horrified eyes. I doubted my overly large crimson irises were of much comfort in this situation, but I returned the stare, gesturing for them to calm down.

"It'll be okay. I'll find a way to fix this!"

I broke my stare and rose to my feet, much to the distress of the Good Personality Half. Their cries of discomfort steadily approached the volume of screams. Guilt tore at my heart, but if I didn't act quickly, a terrible fate would befall us both. Us, and our Person.

I had one idea. I raised a hand over my head and snapped my fingers. "Yo! Penance! Wake up! It's an emergency!"

Dozens of squares formed on the walls, glowing brightly, a faint yellow. They came straight out and hung in midair, forming rows in front of me. I put my finger to the lowest row and swiped right, moving the files accordingly until I came to one labeled *Negative: Disgusts*. One tap dismissed the previous rows and opened Disgusts. Out popped file after file. I grabbed them before they could form a new row and shoved them through the transport slot. It couldn't have been too late for our Person to see them. The thoughts would go through. They had to.

I half-stepped, half-danced over to the screen. The static flickered ... flickered again. Then a full view came to life. I watched as my Person hauled themselves from the floor. They lunged for the toilet and emptied the contents of their stomach. It was disgusting, but I couldn't help the smile tugging at my lips.

"Okay, Tango, everything's fine. I fixed it," I called out as I returned to the open fissure. But as I peered down, it became glaringly obvious everything was not okay.

The Good Personality Half lay motionless on their back, perpetually staring with a dead expression. The light of life had left their eyes, and the dull color in their irises didn't say anything good.

I swallowed all that'd collected in my mouth and shakily rose to a stand. My head shook back and forth, seemingly of its own accord. "No ... No ... This can't be ..."

I was too late?

The floor rumbled underneath my feet. The ceiling collapsed around me and brought the walls down with it. My head forced me to look up, and my body froze. I couldn't move. I couldn't breathe. My eyes were stuck wide as if someone was holding my eyelids with their fingers. I couldn't shake the icy grasp of impending doom crushing my heart.

Beyond the edge of the remaining floor, a skull-faced figure in shadowy robes towered over me. Our gazes met, and his jaw lowered slightly in what I assumed was his best attempt at a smile.

"Pui ... I see your time has come. Your Person was too fragile to withstand the struggles of life any further."

A hot sting plagued my eyes. I couldn't blink it away. My voice ached, screamed, itched to release and say how he was wrong. My Person was strong. My Person had endured for so long. But my lips wouldn't part. My throat wouldn't speak.

The death god rested his cheek in his hand and sighed. "Quite a shame. I sort of liked you. But now is our farewell. I'm sure your Person will find their place among the heavens. I'd prefer they didn't, but merely to console you, I'll say it."

Without another word, he extended his arm and closed his fingers around my body. I could only watch as his face disappeared behind the darkness of his hand. It was then that the affirmation of my fate appeared to me. This was the end.

***

For more information on this author, visit:
pyrakaneauthor.wixsite.com/author

TEXT. AND DRIVE
NERISHA KEMRAJ ⚡

My mom always told me not to text and drive. I should have listened. Now it was too late.

As they wheeled me into the ambulance, I glanced at the mangled red Ford that my VW Polo rammed into. It lay on its roof after flipping over—an absolute wreck. I prayed that everyone was all right, myself included. The lights and sirens dazed me into darkness.

I woke to silence. A sweet smell permeated the room, owing to the flowers on the stand next to me. It was nauseating. The beautiful bouquet accompanied other trinkets of well wishes. They didn't brighten up my mood. Nothing seemed sunny anymore. My head felt heavy, and I could feel the grey clouds hanging above, waiting to release a downpour over me. I couldn't tell which part ached more than the rest. The pain travelled through every inch of my body to an extent where I could no longer tell which was which.

Noticing my moans, my mom awoke from the chair next to me, rushing to my side as I tried and failed to sit up.

"What happened?" I mumbled.

"Shh. It's okay now, Jadie. You'll be all right."

"Why am I in the hospital, Mom?" I asked as fragments of memory from the night before drifted in and out of my mind's eye.

"You were in an accident, sweetheart." Her hands cradled my sore face.

I nestled into her, feeling safe from all the agitation. And then it all came flooding back. Tears gushed down my face, reminding me of the blood that spread across the road. The wreckage. My car, spinning out of control after I swerved into them. Their frightened screams when their car lifted into the air. It seemed to spiral into a never-ending roll before it finally crashed. I watched in horror—ignorant to my own turmoil. I couldn't tear my eyes away until my car came to an abrupt halt after smashing into a tree. So many lives changed. And all that blood.

After a final glance through blurry vision, I noted the empty baby seat from the other car as they carried me onto the stretcher. And then the blaring sirens and bright lights hypnotized me into unconsciousness.

Was there a baby in the car? Were they all right? My head hurt, and it wasn't just from the deep gash that lined my forehead. Reflexively, my hands shot up to my head. Were they alive? I had to find them. I had to make sure they were all okay.

With the memories of the accident came a sudden burst of adrenaline—ripping off the tubes from my nose and those that injected my arms—I struggled out of bed. My mother's efforts to stop me went in vain, but her screams alerted the nurses who subdued me by sedation. Forced into a slumber I could not fight, my heavy eyelids shut the world out, once again.

Once the sedatives wore off, I stayed calm while trying to gain information about the crash victims. I couldn't afford another bout of sedation because I needed to find out what really happened. I had to know.

It was all my fault.

The nurses wouldn't give me much information, and neither would the doctors. I was going in circles, and I felt the walls closing in on me, more each day. My mother said it was out of concern for my health. But they didn't know that not knowing was eating me alive.

Days flew by without any new information. All I was told was that they were a family of three. A two-year-old and her parents. They were apparently "being taken care of," whatever that meant.

I managed to sneak away after finding out their room number. My insides relaxed as my eyes trained on the mother and her daughter who were together in one room. The baby seemed to be perfect in health too. Doe eyes stared up at the ceiling as she mumbled stories to herself. Her cot was free from any tubes and machines. Thankfully, she went unharmed. Tears of relief streaked my face.

Noting the mother asleep, I couldn't keep myself from entering the room. The little baby girl grabbed on to my finger. My heart calmed at her gentle grasp.

"Ello," she began, and I knew I had to leave.

As if sensing my presence, her mother stirred uneasily. I hobbled out of the room as fast as the crutches could carry me. With my heart racing, I could not continue my search for her father as my head wound reminded me that I shouldn't be out of bed. I prayed that he was in as good a condition as they were.

For the first time in thirteen days, I finally slept in peace that night, picturing the angelic face of the little life that was saved.

I was in hospital for just over two weeks, undergoing tests and scans because of my head injury as well as physiotherapy for my broken leg. Doctors said I'll be walking again, it was just a matter of determination and time. The police came by the hospital on the day before my discharge to follow up on the cause of the accident, but I told them I couldn't remember much. It was a serious case, they said. Death was not taken lightly. Death? It was only then that I realised the depth of my callousness; a wife had lost her husband. A daughter lost her father.

A knife pierced through me, scraping across every part of me as the details of that night played over.

I could not breathe.

My mother and I were the only ones that knew what really transpired that night. And now she wouldn't even look at me the same. She tried to hide it, but I could see the disappointment even through the relief of my survival. I'd become a stranger in her eyes. A murderer. I didn't blame her though. How could replying to a text be more important than watching the road?

In a split second, everything changed. It was too late when I looked up from my phone. And in that moment of panic, I tried hitting on the brakes, but my leg found the accelerator instead, resulting in the ruination of so many lives.

Regret flowed through my body as the repercussions of my stupidity were brought to light. Regret was the pounding in my ears as the blood pumped harder while my heart beat faster. I knew it would leap out of my chest at any moment, literally leaving me as heartless as I felt.

Weeks turned into months and still, I could not forget. I had even stalked the funeral. Their images were engraved into my mind. An innocent life taken by my hands.

I couldn't live with myself any more. I couldn't even face myself, so how could I expect others to?

If only I had pulled off to the side of the road and sent that message.

If only I had waited.

If only I had turned my phone off to keep from distracting me.

If only he didn't die.

If only …

His family struggled to move on, and I felt the pain with

them. I had lived a life without a father, and now I had placed that curse on to someone else.

Sitting now in this institution, I deserve so much worse. Two unsuccessful suicide attempts led me to this point. Hopefully, the next time, I'll get lucky. I taste punishment every day, being trapped in the memories of someone else's loss. Mother still comes to visit as much as she can, but things aren't the same anymore … it will never be.

As the nurse leaves me after witnessing me popping the two tiny pills into my mouth, I discretely remove them from under my tongue before they can dissolve. Just a few more weeks, and I'll have enough …

***

For more information on this author, visit:
facebook.com/pg/Nerishakemrajwriter/

TOOTH ⚡
CHRISTINE KING ⚡

Hands on hips, Jade surveyed the scene, listening to the groans. As she turned around, a light dusting of glitter shimmered in the air about her for a moment and then was gone. Signs of carnage were everywhere—splintered chairs, upended tables, shattered glass, and people leaning against walls for support as they gazed around in blank confusion through swollen eyes. Several of those doing the groaning had split lips and swollen or broken jaws. Teeth, blood, and other bodily fluids were sprayed about in a disgusting mural of violence.

With a sigh, Jade stepped towards the long wooden bar, leaving a hint of sparkle, like an iridescent shadow, following her in the gloom of the dirty tavern. She'd never understood why humans thought getting drunk and maiming one another was a fun night out, but she had a clean-up job to do.

Moving carefully, she began picking up the teeth lying in various spots around the room. Some were in easy-to-reach places, others she had to crawl under, over, or around obstacles to get at. She looked up at the ceiling, having learned long ago that teeth could get into very strange places. Sure enough, one was stuck in a high-up tile. A cynical smile spread across her face when she saw it. Bingo!

With a slight shrug of her shoulders, a pair of nearly translucent wings unfurled from her back; they gleamed in the half-light. She wasn't overly concerned about the remaining conscious humans seeing her as she lifted off the ground to retrieve the errant tooth. They were still drunk or concussed from the fight; they would refuse to believe what they saw, and in the cold light of day, think it was no more than a beer-induced hallucination.

Besides, every tooth counted. Expense forms had to be filled out, and these little babies were worth their weight in gold.

When Jade had started as a tooth fairy, it had seemed a fairly simple job. A few nights a week, she went out and collected teeth from under the pillows of children and gave them a standard fee. Then she returned the teeth to the central office and filled out expense forms for each one. The central office paid her commission for each tooth and a very small basic wage.

Unfortunately, they didn't pay her for ripped dresses when windows she had to climb through had nails or bits of wood hanging loose; they didn't pay medical bills if a dog or cat bit or scratched you; and you didn't get danger money for the little brats waking up and calling in Daddy with a baseball bat or—as she remembered on one scary night—a large shotgun.

She had seen it all and been in many situations that no one would believe. After months of hard work with little thanks and even less money, she had sat down and thought hard about her state of affairs. The office wanted teeth, and she knew plenty of places to get them. Bar fights were a good one, but funeral homes usually had corpses lying about. A few teeth are taken, and no one is any the wiser. The same went for morgues and dentist's offices—all easy pickings after her extensive training as a tooth fairy. Locks were not a problem.

Each tooth gained her a payment, and it all helped to pay the rent and hit her quota. Other fairies kept asking what her secret was, but she just shrugged and said, "Hard work." It was true; the cleaning up from fights and even the breaking and entering was all very tiring.

The powers that be never seemed to ask why the teeth she brought in were often bigger or more worn than most baby teeth. The girl on the front desk just took them and counted them before paying up.

Leaving the office, Jade counted her takings for the night and realised she had enough to afford a small meal from her local takeaway. Hiding her wings under her coat, she headed towards the exotic smells coming from her favourite place to eat.

As she walked back into the street with her boxed meal wrapped up in a little bag, she noticed a group of individuals nearby. They paid her no mind, but she watched them enter the local pub and start shouting at someone.

Almost running through her front door, she threw down her coat and grabbed a fork to quickly gobble down her meal—the fight could be starting any minute; she had to time it right. She didn't want to get questioned as a witness.

Throwing her coat back on, glittering with excitement, she almost flew down the stairs from her small apartment and into the pub next door.

Jade bit her lip in frustration at the scene of pleasant, jovial community spirit that greeted her.

Annoyed at the lack of aggressiveness around her, she almost ordered a drink but stopped herself and let her mind work as she eyed up the punters. She sat at a table with an elderly man too drunk to notice her and too busy drinking to care. She looked around the bar and saw a group of men in the corner, maybe the same ones she had seen outside. They were all laughing loudly and seemed to be playing a drinking game. She rolled up her sleeves with a determined expression and headed in their direction.

As the screaming subsided, Jade looked at the blood-splattered walls and felt a small smile play on her lips.

She was impressed by her efforts this evening; after she had tripped a guy and stolen another guy's wallet, the fight had started. The men in the corner had been blamed for the tripping, and the burly guy in the back had been blamed for taking the wallet of the biker at the bar—he had no idea that Jade had planted the wallet on him after removing it from the pocket of its rather scary looking owner. Jade had hidden in the toilets until the fighting finished; stepping out, she tutted at the butchery around her. Blood and teeth everywhere, it was true sometimes it was hard work being a tooth fairy; her small smile turned into a wide grin; she twirled a shimmering twirl; and she started to clean up. Luckily, she didn't mind a bit of hard work.

***

For more information on this author, visit:
christinekingauthor.wixsite.com/mysite

ACOUSTICS
SASHA LAUREN ⚡

"As you can see, Mia, the cathedral ceiling in the kitchen gives it an expansive aura; the duel skylights provide the dining room with ephemerality; the landscaped yard is a haven to relax in after a hard day; the master suite comes complete with a fireplace and spa; the garage allows plenty of space for hodge-podge hobbies; and the recreation room has a full bar with proximity to the whirlpool. I believe this particular house meets all of the requirements you've been looking for in a home."

"Thank you, Mr. Miller. This indeed is the nicest place you've shown me so far. Would you mind if I take a few minutes alone to help me determine if it feels like my home?"

"Certainly, shall I …?"

"Yes, if you don't mind waiting out on the street. I'll come out and meet you when I'm done."

"All right. Have fun."

"I shan't be longer than fourteen minutes."

"Take eighteen if you need."

He tittered, perhaps a bit uncomfortably.

"Thank you, Mr. Miller."

Mia shut the front door, floated through the foyer, and made a beeline to the second floor; she passed through the master suite, into the bathroom, past the bidet, beyond the bowl, and straight to the shower. There, she dropped her bag, pulled out a beige bath sheet, and hung it on the door; she disrobed, watch last.

12:10 p.m., it read.

Leaning in, she adjusted the water temperature—hot, but not scalding. The room began to fill with steam.

She removed bottles of travel shampoo and conditioner from

her bag, stepped inside the silver stall, and sudsed up her hair. With a last adjustment to the water, Mia Chong broke into an up-tempo song, tentatively at first. "*Once a jolly swagman camped by a billabong, under the shade of a coolibah tree. And he sang as he watched and waited 'til his billy boiled. You'll come a-waltzing, Matilda, with me.*"

The acoustics were good!

"*Oh, give me a home where the buffalo roam, where the deer and the antelope play, where seldom is heard a discouraging word, and the skies are not cloudy all day.*"

Fully warmed up now—as much shower dancing as singing, skin warm, lungs warm, heart warm—she chanted resoundingly. "*Om Mani Padme Hum. Om Mani Padme Hum. Om Mani Padme Hum. Om Mani Padme Hum. Auuuuuuum, auuuuuuum, auuuuuuum …*"

She turned the hot to Off, finished with a cold rinse, and hip-hopped out like a newborn bunny. The steamed watch face read: 12:19. True to form, each song had been three minutes.

She adeptly toweled off, combed her shoulder-length, stick-straight, blunted-ended hair, redressed, exited the room, realized she forgot something, re-entered, took her finger, and made a loose jazzy on the steamy mirror.

Mr. Miller looked up from his Scrabble match in which his partner was annoyingly close to closing the gap on his twelve-game lead.

"Ah, twelve twenty-four. Right on time," he intoned as Mia shot energized through the door like the Mad Hatter, late for a very important date.

With her towel draped elegantly over her arm like a waiter at Tavern on the Green, she pumped Joe Miller's clammy hand. "I'll take it!"

THE NOISES THAT QUIET MAKES
KYLE LECHNER

It's so loud downstairs. My parents are yelling and screaming. The noise is so scary. It's scarier than the mean man with the messed-up face and claws in that movie Mommy and Daddy told me I was too little to watch.

I try covering my head with my pillow, but that doesn't help at all. Somebody is breaking something. I hear it shatter. I don't understand why this is happening. Mommy and Daddy never yell. It makes me want to cry, but I know I shouldn't. My dolly tells me it's okay to cry. Dolly says she knows Mommy and Daddy love me no matter what.

I don't want anyone to come upstairs and check on me. I want to pretend I don't exist. Maybe if I wasn't here, Mommy and Daddy wouldn't be yelling. I want to pretend everything I'm hearing downstairs isn't happening. I don't want Mommy and Daddy to yell any more. I don't want to be a reason they are yelling.

It's hard to cry without making any noise. When I try to cry silently, I always end up hiccupping. I don't want to hiccup. I suck a deep breath in and blow it out slow. My crying is caught in my throat, and it feels like it's rattling as it comes out. I stop breathing like that. It's tickling me, and I don't want to cough.

My nose is dripping and stuffed up at the same time. The sleeve of my nightgown is all gross and stringy. I have to pull my hand in and twist my nightgown to wipe my nose with a clean spot. Mommy always tells me, "That's not very lady-like."

It's quiet downstairs now. Maybe, if I pull my blanket over my head and pretend to be asleep, no one will even bother to look in my room. The clock is shining a scary red light through my blanket. It's so late. I have school tomorrow … I mean today. Mommy and Daddy would tell me I shouldn't be up this late. Why does it have to be so loud? Why tonight? Why ever? I've never heard Mommy and Daddy yell like this. At least they aren't yelling now. But I wonder what were they yelling about?

This blanket is making it too hard to breathe. Someone is moving downstairs. It's the same sounds I hear when it's Christmas and Santa is putting presents under the tree. They are trying to be quiet, but quiet has its own noises. There is someone on the steps now. I don't want them to look in my room. I just want to disappear until morning.

Maybe I should hide in the closet. But then they wouldn't see me sleeping and might come in my room. I know. If I move my pillows and cover them with my blanket, it will look like I'm sleeping. Maybe then no one will come in, and I can still feel safe in my hiding place.

The closet is dusty and dark and lonely. Dolly is still on my bed. She says to leave her with pillow-me and watch through the slats of the closet door. Dolly promises she'll protect me and that the best way she can is to make them think pillow-me is me-me.

Mommy and Daddy's door squeaks as it opens. It makes this loud, scary creak. They are moving around an awful lot in there. *Please don't come in my room.* Please. Tears start flooding my eyes again. I don't want to cry, but I can't stop myself. Trying to cry quietly is hard. It tickles my throat. It feels like I'm trying to swallow a cotton ball. I grab my jacket that's hanging beside me and cough into it.

My door creaks open. Two people come into my room. That's not Mommy and Daddy. Those are strangers. They go to my bed and rip the blanket off. Dolly doesn't even move. She must be too scared. She stares at the closet and tells me not to make a sound. I nod and try to stop crying. I hiccup.

The two men stop tearing apart my room and turn to the

closet door. I shove my snot-covered sleeve in my mouth and hold my breath to stop the next hiccup. It doesn't work. My back hits the back of the closet, and my coats fall in front of me like a curtain. My heels feel hot from the rug burn I just got scooting backwards so fast.

Another hiccup forces its way up my throat. My closet door flies open. Dolly screams that she's sorry as my hangers squeak on the bar above my head. I hiccup, and a man I don't know looks down at me. A shriek tears itself free from my throat and leaves it ragged and hoarse. My scream breaks my ears. The only reason I know the stranger is speaking is because his cracked and filthy lips are moving.

Tears and snot and wet coughs bubble out of me and burst. Mommy and Daddy are yelling again from downstairs. Flashing lights outside my window fill my room with long colorful shadows. One of the men runs to the window but stumbles when Dolly reaches out and trips him. The sound of him hitting the glass makes me flinch. The other stranger keeps staring at me like I'm going to tell him the best place he can hide. He breaks away from the door and runs to look out the window too. Their boots sound like thunder as they storm around my room yelling at each other while I'm trying to disappear back into my coats.

All I can think to do is squeeze my eyes shut and pretend I don't exist. Everything is so loud that it all blends together. My throat is hoarse, and my face is streaked and tacky. I'm breathing like I forgot how. A hammering in my chest rattles my head and makes stars burst behind my eyelids.

Pinching my eyes shut hurts too much. Everything is spinning when I ease them open. Dolly has been trampled on and is crying on the floor. The lights are still flashing outside my window. All I can hear now are the noises that quiet makes.

Someone is coming up the stairs.

***

For more information on this author, visit:
facebook.com/BrokenSpines13

THE ABORTION
R. ROY LUTZ

It was on Jenny's fourteenth birthday when she went to the clinic with her mother. She was afraid.

Her mother's voice quavered. "You know, it doesn't hurt. You step into the chamber and zap, it's over. The director says there are too many mouths."

She knew it was for the best, but a tear trickled down Jenny's cheek. The doctor was reassuring. They signed the papers. Her mother kissed her before closing the chamber door.

A flash of light signaled the end of a life.

It's just me now, Jenny thought as she walked alone out of the clinic.

***

For more information on this author, visit:
facebook.com/R.RoyLutzTheAuthor

ADA & JOYCE
CATHERINE A. MACKENZIE

When alive, I had always wondered if I would see those pearly gates supposedly protecting the entrance to Heaven.

I had successfully travelled through the tunnel, that long winding laneway with enticing radiant lights that beckoned like a glowing pot of gold at the end of the rainbow. Surprisingly, the gates were there, gleaming white, spread wide. They weren't formed of pearls but were inviting nonetheless, like the proverbial white picket fence. Of course, special permission had to be granted to approach. God doesn't allow just anyone to enter His kingdom; one has to be good and worthy.

I was met at that mythical gold pot by a gentleman in a long, flowing robe. White, of course. Everything in Heaven, I discovered, was embraced in white.

After settling into my new home, I answered the knock on the door.

"Hi," the woman said, squinting at me. Surprise flickered over her face. "Ada?"

"Joyce? When did you get here?"

"Just arrived. I heard there was someone new from Bakersfield, so I thought I'd come see who it was. Wasn't expecting you."

"I didn't know you were here, either," I said.

"Nice place, eh? Way nicer than I expected. Quite lovely."

"Yes, everyone frets over the afterlife. Too bad we don't know beforehand what to expect. Living would be easier, that's for sure. What happened to you, Joyce? Why are you here?"

"I froze to death."

"What! How horrible," I said.

I didn't want to be rude and ask what happened. I hadn't seen much of Joyce during the last couple of years. At the frozen comment, I quickly surmised she had developed Alzheimer's, escaped from a nursing home, and perished outdoors in the snow. Or perhaps she had wandered to the cemetery to pay respects to her late husband, Edmund, and keeled over before freezing by his grave.

Joyce glanced at me before continuing. "It wasn't that bad. It was very cold at first, then I kind of became numb like I was hot. Then I was sleepy. I don't remember anything after that. Until I found myself in the tunnel heading to the pearly gates. What about you? How did you die?"

"I had a heart attack."

"Oh, now that is more horrible, I would think. The pain and all," Joyce said.

"No, it was quite painless, actually. And probably self-induced," I said.

"What do you mean by that? How could you cause your own heart attack?" Joyce rubbed her smooth face.

Joyce never seemed to age, and I'd always been jealous of her. Though a couple of years older than me, she appeared at least ten years younger. I wasn't sure what she did to keep herself looking so good. She must have had surgery or frequent doses of Botox.

"I thought Harold was cheating on me," I replied.

"Oh my!" Joyce gasped, and her hand flew to her mouth. "Cheating? Harold?"

"Yeah, a suspicion I had. I came home early one night from my crochet circle to hopefully catch him in the act. I was positive he was with someone. But when I came in, he was in the den watching TV. I searched everywhere. In our bedroom. Under our bed. In our closet. I even checked the other bedrooms. My granddaughter Abby hides behind the drapes in the dining room when she plays hide and seek, so I checked there too. Nope. No one."

I paused. Joyce's eyes bore into mine.

I continued with my story. "I raced around the entire house, determined to find the bitch. My heart sped a million miles a minute, along with a myriad of thoughts. My legs were killing me from all the frantic running. Finally, the stress got to me, I guess. The last thing I remember was falling to the floor. I hope Harold tried to bring me back to life, but …"

Thinking of my Harold cheating on me brought back too many awful memories, and I desperately tried to hold back tears.

"Haha."

Joyce's snickering pissed me off. How could someone laugh about that—and at my expense? The episode caused my death, after all, without a dire consequence to Harold. In fact, he was probably relishing his new existence without me.

"Promise you won't be mad if I tell you something?" Joyce tittered again. "Not that it matters. There's no promises or madness in Heaven. All's fun and giggles." To prove her point, she laughed once more. "Actually, I should be mad at you."

"Mad at me? What did I do?" I was dumbfounded she'd be angry with me—and in Heaven, no less. What happened to forgiveness?

She glanced at me before staring into space. "When you were searching the house for the so-called other woman, you should have looked in the deep freeze. Perhaps we'd both be alive if you had." Joyce giggled. "At least, I would have been. You might still have died from your heart attack. Oh my word, you should have seen Harold and I scurry around when we saw your call pull up. 'The deep freeze,' he said. 'Jump in.' I didn't want to, of course. I hate the cold." As if remembering, she crossed her arms across her pointy boobs and rubbed her arms. "Gah, how I hate the cold. But we had no choice. Everything happened so fast, and I never dreamt I'd be in there that long." Her eyes darkened. "That damn man. Why didn't he come save me? He should have known I couldn't last forever in there."

"Yeah, well, did he try to save me?"

Joyce squinted "How would I know?"

"I like to think he tried to save me, but perhaps he let me die so he could have you."

Joyce glared at me for a second until her face lit up. "But I died too. Haha, isn't that hilarious? We both died, so he was left with no one! Serves him right, eh?" She laughed even harder then, huge guffaws so laborious she bent over and massaged her too-flat stomach. "Oh, my belly. Hurting so bad."

It was my turn to clench my aching belly. I was in Heaven—right?—where there is no pain, only fun and laughter. "Yes, we snookered him, didn't we?"

And then we hugged and giggled.

***

For more information on this author, visit: writingwicket.wordpress.com

LIVIA'S DADDY COMES HOME FROM THE WAR

JAN MAHER

June 1945

Mama's acting funny. It's not Sunday and she makes me and Jed put on Sunday clothes. And I have to put my paper dolls away and just sit on the Davenport and look at my picture book. And Jed has to comb his hair. Mama tucks his shirt in and he asks why and she says someone special is going to be here. And there's a knock and she says he's here and a man walks into the room in funny clothes. His shirt and pants are muddy color, and a hat like none I ever seen. It's the same color too. Greeny brown. And she kisses him. The only time I ever seen her kiss a man was New Year's Eve, they hung a thing in the doorway and my Uncle Jake standed under it and they made us all kiss him, even Gramma kissed him and my cousin Luzy who is more little than me. I'm almost five and she's three and a brat.

Mama kisses him a long one. He acts like he doesn't see me or Jed till that's over. Then he sticks his hand out to Jed like he's grownup or something, even though he's nine and a pain, and says hi son how ya doing. Jed gets red and shuffles his feet. He says fine so quiet I almost can't hear him say it and Mama just smiles like it's Christmas which it isn't, it's the day before my birthday. I'm almost five and Christmas was before Easter.

And Jed shakes his hand. And then he asks me can he have a kiss. I'm not spose to kiss people I don't know. I'm looking at his feet and not his eyes. I watched his eyes when he shaked Jake's hand. His eyes are crinkly and I don't like that. Livia, Mama says, Livia, it's your daddy come home from the war, you can kiss him hello, he's your daddy. He's home now.

I chew on the inside part of my lip and I look up at his

crinkly-eyed old face and I say loud that isn't my daddy. He doesn't look like that. He doesn't wear them funny clothes. Then Jed hits me on the head with his knuckles and it hurts so I kick him but he gets away. Dummy he says. That's just his uniform. That's just your uniform, ain't it Dad Jed says with a stupid grin just cause he thinks he's hot stuff just cause he's four years older.

Mama says Jed keep your hands off your sister and the man laughs ho ho ho like them Santa Clauses they got at Christmas at all the stores and I don't think they are really Santa Clauses cause there's only one of him. And he's sposed to be making things. This man here laughs like that and Mama says you probly don't member him you were just a baby when he went overseas. Nu uh, I was one, I say and besides my daddy's in France I say. I stick my lip out 'cause I know I'm right. He sent me shoes for Easter and I pull my dress up to show them.

He says they are pretty and I can tell he never seen them before. If you never seen them before you can't be my daddy I say. Mama, I say, he can't be my daddy. I showed it.

She's pretty smart he says and Jed says smart mouth dumb head and Mama says shut up Jed. I sent your mama money, he says, and she got you the shoes. I stick my lip out at Mama, you said my shoes came from my daddy in France. Mama says the money came from France and I say you said the shoes came from France and then I am quiet. I'm thinking what other lies did she tell me? Do you want to see some French money he says and he puts his hand in his pocket and pulls out two things like pennies and he gives me one and Jed one.

Then Jed goes jumping on him, did you bring me anything from the war he says. Ho ho ho says the man, what sort of things do you want? A gun Jed says. Ho ho ho they don't let you take guns home from the war. You can have my canteen. Where is it Jed yells. I'll get it for you in a minute he ho hos. First I want a hug from my Livia. I'm not your Livia I say.

Ho ho ho, come here a minute the man says I'll let you wear my hat and he puts the greeny brown thing on my head. I throw it on the floor. Then Jed says can I have it Daddy and the man looks at it and looks at me and looks at Jed and looks at me and Jed goes to pick it up and I grab it. No he says J-boy, the hat is for Livia. I want my canteen says Jed can you get it now?

I'll get it now he says and turns away from looking at me.

I'm membering hard now looking at his back but I can't member about this man. I member a man in France who sended me shoes but now I can't member what he's sposed to look like. He puts his hand in his big greeny brown bag and pulls out another greeny brown thing that's round. Everything about him is greeny brown. Here you go, J-boy, you can keep this. Use it if you ever go fishing or camping. Jed says can I have the hat too, Daddy? Please? Livia don't want it.

I hold the hat with both my hands. The man says no J-boy, I'll find you some other things. First I want to get out of these clothes. Don't ever want to wear them again, he says.

Why not Daddy, Jed's looking at him funny and Mama is too, different from Jed. Mama's crying, I know 'cause I can see her face is wet. I never seen her cry before.

Cause the war is over the man says. I don't ever want to fight another one.

Not ever says Jed isn't war fun?

The man gets a funny look on his face too and Mama says you go play now J-boy. Daddy's going to change into see villyun clothes.

What's that, says Jed.

Like what you're wearing, says the man. Just regular clothes. I don't ever want to wear these ugly things again.

Well, just there he knows they're ugly. I'm glad he knows that. He looks at me again and says after I get my clothes changed I want you to tell me what you want for your birthday tomorrow.

He knows that too!

I don't know now. Maybe he is my daddy. I sure don't member him like this. Then he goes into my mama's bedroom, with his big greeny brown bag. She goes in too and she shuts the door. Jed goes into the kitchen and puts water in the round thing.

I watch Mama's door and practice saying to myself my daddy's home from the war.

My daddy's home from the war.

***

For more information on this author, visit: janmaher.com

THE CASE ⚡
JACOB MAICHEL

It happened again yesterday. Some unlucky bastard disappeared. Like usual, the news blew through town. Bill or Bob maybe, hell who cared what his name was, only that he had a wife. Probably a kid and mortgage too. Every year like clockwork the disappearances would occur; death season they called it. Always the same dark shadows in the sky and then there would be disappearances. His brother had been abducted last year. His sister-in-law the year before that; although, he hadn't been as broken up about the ole battle axe.

He couldn't worry about it now though; he was late for work. Punctuality hadn't been Jim's thing lately, and he knew it would catch up to him soon. Before, as detective, he had enjoyed some flexibility when it came to work hours, but that had been over a year ago. Some hard cases had led to drinking, demotion, and missing the time clock on a regular basis. The doc had put "lacks anger control, mixed with tendencies toward addiction" in his file, and like that, poof, his time on the street disappeared. Either way, he no longer worked cases; now he ran a desk. Hell, at least he had a drawer for his whisky.

The precinct bustled with activity. As he came through the door, it reminded him of a swarm of some gnats hovering just above the water right before a fish made lunch of the idiots. As he pushed through *heys* and *good mornings* and hit the floor with little to no notice.

Nearing the desk, though, the duty officer looked pissed. What's new? He always looked pissed. "Jim, you're late!" he shouted across the room louder than needed—he was a drunk, not deaf. "The captain wants you in his office."

"What does he want, Mort?"

"How the hell should I know. Do I look like your message service?"

"No, Mort. You look like you got a corn cob or bug up your arse, and it's compounded by underwear a size to small."

"Jim, you ain't drunk again, are ya?"

"Nope, but the day is young."

The captain's office door down the hall stood open.

"Sit down, Mills!"

Jim knew it had to be bad if the old man had been waiting for him. The smell of cigars and joint salve permeated every pore of the office, bringing imagines of locker rooms with athletes past their prime.

"Sit!" It came more as a grunt.

Man, he didn't have the level of caring for this crap.

"What do you know about the disappearances, Mills?"

"Not much. They happen mostly in the spring and summer, and what few witnesses we have say some babblings about individuals being pulled up into the sky."

"You're close on most of it, Mills. The main things you're missing are juveniles are sent back, and the group that is targeted seems to change depending on what time of year it is."

"What's your point, Captain? Crap happens, and people disappear. You got a point, Cap?"

"Mills, I need new eyes on the case, and you're it. You're promoted temporarily back to detective."

"I haven't worked a case in over a year. Can't you grab Wilson?"

"Wilson was abducted last week; no, Jim, it is you. Look, Mills, I know you had a rough patch, but this one is from up top, and neither one of us has a choice. Interview some of the families, work the case, see if anything shakes loose. Now, get out before I decide to fire you instead."

The files were thick. For years, the department had been working the disappearances, and now they had an entire room dedicated to the reams of notes and evidence. It took one look at the room before he decided that was not what he wanted this morning. He would take the captain's advice and go visit the victims. They all had the same story, just different names—so-and-so had been going somewhere and never made it. The young ones were even more confusing. They would be pulled into the sky and grabbed by giants, then dropped back to the ground. Like *Jack and the Beanstalk.* He knew that could not be right; it sounded like one of those late-night shows on near-death experiences.

Still feeling effects of the cheap whiskey he'd embalmed himself with the night before, he needed some hair of the dogfish to clear his mind. The bartender at the local watering hole agreed that the stories were farfetched; he probably just left to get away from a crazy woman. The bartender—a fellow by the name of Vinny—for the "record" stated, "Eh, dey leave. What's da mystery?" but poured the drinks all the same.

Hell, the next step would be to stake out an area high in disappearances and wait. The spot had seen several occurrences this month; if he would find anything, it should happen here. Jim watched the picturesque view of the countryside, feeling the stress and drinking away. He'd had a wife once—strong swimmer, pretty eyes. He took stock of everything; where had it gone wrong? Captain had given him the case because he was dispensable more than new eyes or whatever crap he'd been given. Sitting lost in thought, something grabbed his attention. What the hell?

In the distance, he could make something out; it shimmered and seemed to be moving. It gave him pause; it looked alien. It stirred something in him, bringing out animalistic urges. *I am a cop, damn it.* He fought the need to charge to it. He wanted out of the situation. Waves of memories from old cases came rushing in. *I haft to investigate!* He willed himself to go calmly to see what it was that appeared to hang in midair.

As he got closer, he could see that it was metallic and rod-shaped, in a curved almost *C* shape. It was writhing, though alive, and someone or something had pierced a living thing through the body with this ... hook and impaled the animal with it. What was it? A worm? It screamed and cried out as he got closer; obviously, this thing's mind was gone. He wanted it to stop and the worm to shut up and the hook to disappear—it felt wrong, so wrong!

He closed in quickly. As he got to the worm, a terrible thought washed over Jim. *You haven't had breakfast.* No, he could not. This worm had been tortured, had been impaled like kabob. Still, he craved him, needed to taste him. *No!*

"Hold still! I'm trying to help you off, man."

He could get a good grip, if he would just hold still. What the hell? The hook had a wire or string attached to it. Who would do this?

"Just kill me!"

"I'll get you off, man. We'll get you help. Calm down."

Visions of eating the worm washed over him again and again. *No, I can't. I am a cop. I save. I don't eat the victims.* Things were bad, Jim knew it. He pulled on the worm again, screams erupted.

"What the hell!"

He needed a drink, craved food. He felt helpless, then ... *Gulp.* The screaming had stopped. He couldn't believe it. No, no, no. Had he eaten the worm? God, he needed a drink. He had to report it. Now there was another issue; the hook had lodged itself into his mouth. He turned and thrashed, but the ... the hook pulled back with a sudden jerk.

"What the fucking hell?"

He yanked his head back, but the hook pulled him closer

and closer to the sky. He could see like a film. What was that? Then he was through.

"Dang, Bob, you got yourself a big one there."

"Heck ya I do, Herald. That's an eight or even nine pounder. Good cooking too."

"He swallowed your hook though."

"Yeah, it's them nightcrawlers. They can't resist 'em."

The giant that had been called "Bob" stood over Jim and reached into his mouth with some large metal device and yanked. His insides were ripped out, pain tearing through him. Blood trickled from his mouth.

"Throw 'em in the bucket. We'll clean him later, Bob."

For a brief moment, as he flew through the air, hope bloomed till he landed in the bucket with four others. Some of the more enlightened giants over the years may have wondered what a creature like Jim thought as he was pulled from the bucket and watched the knives come out. Jim's thoughts, however, were simple and to the point.

Well, crap. I can't believe my last meal was a dirty-ass worm.

FLASH ⚡
TOM MOHLER

They say your life flashes before your eyes just moments before your impending death. Some glorious vision laid out in front of you for a split-second right before you meet your maker. A recollection of all your accomplishments, your triumphs.

Here I am, leaning against the wall of this crumbling apartment complex, a gun in my mouth and blood pooling around my feet. As I tongue the muzzle, all I can taste is the freshly burnt powder. The warmth of the still smoking barrel resting between my lips lets me know that I'm still alive.

Through the ringing in my ears, I can hear feverous yelling that constantly grows louder. Thundering footsteps that are closing in on my position. The sounds of strife that I am all too familiar with. Their source will soon to be upon me.

I just wanted a normal life. I just wanted to do my part. And I did. More than you could ever know.

At this moment, all I want is salvation. Forgiveness. Everlasting peace.

I'm wearing the last uniform that I will ever need. Wishing that a life full of accomplishments and great victories would flash before my eyes, but here I am, drawing a blank. Just a solitary security guard assigned to some bleak section-eight housing project on the graveyard shift.

My peace-time security detail back in the world.

A life spent in conflict can teach you many things. Out of the womb and into the real shit. You graduate high school and jump right into the service of one nation, under some leader, who thinks he's God. That is the life that you've chosen. Do it for honor. Do it for your country. Become a man among men.

You learn a lot about yourself when an enemy insurgent slips out from behind cover and you quickly plant that glowing red chevron onto his body and squeeze the trigger. A short burst of gunfire sent screaming into the upper chest of a man will end a confrontation in the blink of an eye. Ask anyone in the know. They'll tell you. Just a spurt of red mist, and the body hits the dirt. A clean kill.

This is war. This is my purpose. It is what I was trained to do. This is not the real world. That is what you tell yourself.

Sometimes a child with an explosive strapped to their chest comes charging out of an alleyway towards you and your squad mates. And sometimes you have to kill a child without hesitation. The trigger clicks, the hammer drops, and a copper-plated lead projectile of righteous judgment soars through the air, eliminating the one whom wishes us harm.

A child dies so that we may continue to live. It was either him or us. There was no other option. That is what you tell yourself.

The truth is that war is hell. The battlefield, hell on earth. In that place, you are not yourself. You must act as judge, jury, and executioner at a moment's notice, without hesitation and without regret. You are the angel of death. Once that's ingrained into you, it never goes away. No matter how much you want to leave it behind, it is always with you. It becomes you.

A life spent in hell conditions you. It creates you. It prepares you to come back to the world to live a life of despondence, constantly tormented by the ghosts you've created. Prepares you to wake up in a cold sweat every single night as you're suffocated by the gruesome images of dismembered bodies burned into your subconscious.

This is why you work a shit security job for a slave's wage on the graveyard shift in some dingy Section 8-housing project. This is what makes you act on instinct when someone behind you shouts, "Stick em' up, asshole!"

All rational thought goes out the window as your muscle memory kicks in. You draw your weapon and quickly turn to meet your assailant, pulling the trigger as the threat enters your sights, just as you've done so many times before. It's not until right after that heated moment of swift, precise violence that you realize what you've done. That you've just collapsed the chest cavity of a twelve-year-old boy holding a squirt gun.

You did this just as you had done to countless enemy combatants before him. Lights out in the blink of an eye. You did your part. Those expertly placed rounds did exactly what was intended of them. This is all proof of your elite training. Threat engagement 101.

The young boy's body lies on the ground beside me. Slumped over and motionless, resting in an ever-growing sea of his own mortality. The orange water pistol still clenched in his hand. There was no scream. Just a loud bang, a bright flash, and some red mist followed by his body hitting the floor.

I know that this is the point of no return. This is not the battlefield, this is the real world. Brutal and honest. I am alone in the universe, my back against the wall. Covered in a child's blood whose name I will never know, a smoking gun planted firmly in my mouth. Sitrep: conditions unfavorable.

Praying that some glorious vision of all my life's accomplishments would come bursting through my mind before the inevitable blackness. Desperate to find meaning in an existence willingly sold into unquestioning service. Begging for something, anything at all to flash before my eyes.

That's when it hits me. The vision that I've been so desperately seeking. The cold hard truth of it all.

I have been molded into a tool of warfare, one that could never hope to reintegrate with the real world. I could never lead the so-called normal life that I so deeply desire. I have been trained to pull the trigger in the face of adversity, to act on instinct without remorse and without falter. That is my inescapable destiny. That is my life's grand accomplishment. Some create, and I destroy.

This is what I have become. It is who I am. Wrath incarnate.

The blaring commotion has grown so loud that I can make out some garbled words amidst the chaos. A man shouts, "That gah'dam rent-a-pig shot somebody!" Another voice quickly follows: "Get that son'ova bitch!" The thundering footsteps stampeding down the hallway are seconds from reaching me. With all this noise pouring into my still ringing ears, I know that it's time for immediate evac.

Acceptance is the end. Accept your fate. Accept your destiny. It's yours. Own it.

As I begin to squeeze the trigger, I think to myself, *May God have mercy on my soul.*

A soul. I hope I still have one.

Click.

Bang.

Flash.

Red mist.

Lights out.

ALBATROSS
ELIZABETH MONTAGUE

The thunderous roar of heavy artillery rings out overhead, shaking the walls around us, dust raining down from months of neglect. The tiny viewing ports are lit for a moment with a flash of fire that is quickly extinguished by the driving rain. A cloying, metallic smell that always accompanies an assault mixes with sweat—born of fear and weeks without adequate sanitation. We're stewing in the bags of our uniforms, the material able to keep out stray bullets, but it keeps everything in as well. We all stink, but it's the least of our worries.

One of the rookies—Mason, I recall—shrieks and then laughs at herself as a particularly loud boom shakes us harder. The enemy fire becoming more precise. Several more giggle at the reaction, but I know they're all as scared as each other. My unit is in its second rotation to the front. Eighteen of us from the original group returning with twenty-two new soldiers, some experienced, some green. We all wear scars. Not a single person doesn't relive the fight night after night. My own dreams still have me screaming. I shrug them off. I have to fight.

The commander comes in, and everyone's attention is turned to him, ears pricked for instructions whilst the uncertain ones fiddle with their boot straps. It won't be long now until we go. My fingers itch, and I shift them away from the trigger of my gun.

Another shell shakes our bunker, and even I flinch at the noise of it. Soon we'll be out there again. Soon we'll take back the stronghold they stole from us in their last offensive. We can't let them gain any more ground. We have to win.

I see the determination on the faces of the soldiers around

me, the older ones serving as my mentors for many years. They'd laughed at me when I had hurried to enlist at eighteen; they'd schooled me with tough love when I had first seen the world above the bunkers; they'd taken me as their sister in arms when I had fought beside them.

Ferguson was my captain at my first rotation, and I've returned to serve him again. He was the one that held me fast when I'd seen the grey, flattened world outside. I had grown up on tales of the lush, green land that had existed before the war, before our weapons destroyed it all. The bleak view was testament to the life we now lived. No side was ever going to win, but we kept on at each other all the same. Somewhere we had forgotten what had started the fighting, but we knew we couldn't let them win. Alliances were made and broken. Friends became enemies. Countries were torn to pieces as we sheltered in the strongholds beneath the ground, living our half-life. Ferguson told me that at least if I was fighting I would be able to see what was left of the sky.

The stink of fried metal seeps through the air vents, the shell that made us all jump having hit close enough to burn out several filters. Wide-eyed rookies reach for their gas masks, and the vets laugh them off. I join the laughter, but the sound is forced. If the bullets don't get you the gas might. It's always the gas in the end. For all our advances in technology, the old ways still come to the fore. When our defence system nullified their missiles before they hit the ground and theirs did the same to ours, we all went back to the bullet, the blade, the toxic gas. We had come no further in two hundred years from those bloodied soldiers in the trenches of the Great War.

Those men are legends now, held up like Arthurian knights, legends of old. Now there are no heroes. Everything is futile.

When they landed on the beaches on D-Day they gave them great names. Utah, Omaha, Gold, Sword, Juno. Strong, powerful names. We've since lost our gravitas to necessity. So many raids needing names, so many beaches, trenches, land grabs. They tried to keep them sensible, but ideas began to run dry. Now our units are named after birds, and the missions are equally ridiculous.

"Albatross unit. Prepare to execute mission to Banana Bunker." The commander barks the order, and we're all on our feet in a second.

A couple of the rookies laugh, but those who have been out there before grit their teeth. Ridiculous as the names are, the bloodshed is not. If you die on a mission to reclaim Banana Bunker, you die. It won't matter that the name was stupid.

"Let's get the bastards." Ferguson's voice rouses me, and I remember that I am a soldier. I remember the lives the enemy stole when they stormed the bastion three days before.

The whistle sounds. We run out of the reinforced bunker and into the vast grey expanse that is No Man's Land. Land too scarred and barren from the bombings to be worth anything other than inches to our opposing sides. We slog through mud and the rot of a thousand bodies that no one could bury, and all the while, craters continue to open up around us, heavy artillery raining down.

Screams mingle with the dull thuds, and my dreams play out before me again as a bomb strikes, blowing away Mason. The rookie laughing no more. She didn't even make it to Banana Bunker.

An eerie silence seems to fall even though our soldiers are still screaming. A buzzing sounds overhead, and we all know it's too late to go back. We push forward in the hope of reaching shelter before the gas hits, masks too restrictive to wear in the field despite the risk.

The buzzing stops. It's too late.

I keep running even as the gas hits, my throat scratching on every breath, but it's better than the searing pain that follows. I choke on my own blood as the soft tissue is stripped bare. I gasp for air, but it doesn't get past the flood in my lungs. My eyes are next. The world grows dark, but I keep stumbling through the bombardment. I know the wetness on my cheeks isn't blood or sweat, it's my eyeballs melting from their sockets. I'm dying. The bullets don't matter.

I'm dying.

With all that's left in me, I stumble forward. I trip, the pain merely adding to the agony as I hit the floor, but my hand strikes metal. I made it. The victory is pointless though. If I could speak, my last words would be nonsense.

"Albatross. Banana."

***

For more information on this author, visit:
facebook.com/elizabethmontaguewrites

CIMMERIAN SHADE
T.C. MORGAN

"Time for bed, Lorn," Rebec called out to her six-year-old son.

The boy huffed but picked up his toy and headed in her direction.

"Loccam," she said anxiously, and her eyes met with those of her husband's.

He was checking all of the locks in the home, making sure that they were securely in place. His eyes drifted to the large minute counter that was built into the wall. A second misplaced could mean the difference between life and death. Loccam put on a smile that he didn't feel and nodded to his wife. They were both relatively young, but crows' feet had begun taking up residence at the corners of her eyes, and his forehead was lined.

While Loccam finished securing the home, Rebec went about setting up the shadow tent that would shield them while they slept. She feared the dark but feared what lived just outside of it even more. That spurred on her fingers as she anchored the tent into the slats of the floor.

Her young son lay on the bed, playing with his stuffed toy and singing a song to himself. Rebec smiled, knowing that he had no concept of the danger that he and every other person left alive on Earth was in. Once the sides of the tent were secured, she looked at the thin watch on her wrist, and her anxiety began to rise again.

"Loccam, it's ten forty-five. Come to bed so we can get the Cimmerian shade going."

Loccam eyed the latches of the home one more time, making sure that they were in the locked position before heading into the bedroom. He bolted the room door and, as always, pushed the heavy wedge he'd fashioned out of cement and metal in front of it. That never stopped them from getting in, but Loccam had made it his life's work to find something that could at least secure one room in the house.

He sighed, but once he saw the look of stress and fear on his wife's face, he smiled again. "Hey babe, you get under the covers with Lorn. I'll put the Cimmerian shade up."

Rebec nodded, and sliding under the comforters, she cuddled their son in her arms. This was the part that she hated most. The lights had already been dimmed after they'd had dinner, leaving their black-painted home in the shadows. But, once Loccam turned on the Cimmerian shade, it would deflect all light away from them. Within the little tent that was only big enough to cover their bed, they'd be engulfed by darkness.

The tent moved as Loccam checked around it, making sure that it was securely in place. He was a thorough man when it came to his family and wanted to leave nothing to chance. When he seemed sure of it, he climbed inside the tent with his young son and wife. Rebec had made it no secret to him that she was afraid of the dark and, as always, he took her hand in his while the other held the Cimmerian shade. He gave her a tired but reassuring smile, waiting for her assent to turn the device on.

Rebec closed her eyes and held onto Lorn as he nuzzled closer to her. The dark didn't seem too bad a thing behind closed eyelids. But, when she nodded to her husband, she got the same rude awakening that she always did.

The bed shifted as Loccam hung the Cimmerian shade from the top of the closed tent. When he activated it, the device ate up all the light within a twelve-foot radius, leaving them in an inky darkness that mirrored midnight in a cave.

She held onto Lorn, and Loccam spooned her from behind.

"Mama," Lorn whispered sleepily, "where do the Rouksascs come from?"

"Nobody knows, baby," she said as she smoothed his dark hair away from his tired face. "Some think the space probe that came back from Mars two hundred years ago brought them here. Others think they've been here all along but someone or something woke them up."

"What do they look like?"

Rebec thought about the tall, slender creatures with rounded heads and sharp teeth that could crunch through bone. Their flesh reeked of rotting fish and secreted a slimy essence that was left behind wherever they went.

"They are gray," she said carefully, "and icky. But, let's talk about something else, Lorn. I don't want to give you nightmares."

"Eleven o'clock," Loccam said gently. "Time for bed."

Lorn began drifting off to sleep, but Rebec was wide awake. It always took some doing for her to get to sleep. Loccam would offer his help, which usually came in the form of holding her until morning. Soon though, it was midnight.

Rebec heard them as they entered the home.

No one knew how they got in. Since houses were kept necessarily dark, cameras were useless in tracking their movements. Loccam would spend his days reinforcing the heavy metal barriers and his evenings barricading the windows, but both were always fruitless ventures.

Something crashed to the floor in the kitchen, and Rebec flinched.

"Shh," Loccam whispered reassuringly in her ear.

The creatures didn't care about, nor hunt by sound. It was sight that drove them. Having eyes that picked up light on all spectrums, the only way to truly stay protected from their ravenous appetites was to remain in complete darkness. The Rouksascs only hunted at night, so there was relative safety during waking hours. But, when the moon was high, they came out in droves.

Rebec kept a clean home, so she knew that there wasn't any paper or debris on the floor of her room. Despite that, she heard something like a food wrapper being crushed underfoot near their bed. Her hold on their son tightened when the smell of rancid fish wafted up her nostrils.

The floor creaked beneath the weight of the creatures that slowly slinked around the bedroom. There was a clicking sound as the Rouksascs' eyes adjusted to the darkness. It never escaped her knowledge that the only thing separating her family from death by evisceration was the thick fabric that they were encased by and the small device that enveloped them in blackness. The sound of angry hissing and claws scraping let her know that not only would she have to clean extensively once the sun came out, she'd have to spackle the walls of their room too.

Then, the tent moved.

Lorn was sound asleep, but that didn't stop Rebec from clamping her hand over his mouth. She did the same to herself, afraid that if she even whimpered in fear, the creatures might hear. Loccam was awake as well and stiffened beside her. He hugged her tightly one last time before slowly rolling over and picking up the rifle that they kept hidden in the wooden railing of their bed. Rebec knew that if he had to protect his family, Loccum would probably only get one shot off before being attacked, and there were at least three Rouksascs in the room.

The angry tugging at the tear-resistant tent continued, but the fabric held up. The Cimmerian shade, however, began to rattle above them from the constant movement. Rebec shuttered in fear as tears fled silently from her eyes.

She didn't want to know what it felt like to have her child ripped from her arms and broken open like a nut before her eyes. She didn't want to see the fear and defeat on her husband's face when the last thing he saw was his family being devoured alive. She didn't want to know what it felt like to be torn open and eaten like a starving man ravishing a melon.

The darkness of the tent prevented her from seeing what was going on outside of it, but the beasts seemed to give up. The tugging stopped, and the sound of more things breaking around the home could be heard as they made their speedy exit. That was their way. No one knew how they got in, and although they made a good amount of noise, no one knew how they left either.

Both she and her husband lay in bed, holding hands but saying nothing. Loccam still had the rifle beside him, ready to use it but relieved that he didn't have to. Rebec's hold on Lorn loosened slightly, and the boy rolled over, blissfully unaware of what had nearly happened.

It was still another five hours or so until the sun rose again, and Rebec's body shook from misplaced adrenaline and fatigue. Her family was safe, but she knew that someone else's that night wouldn't be, and tomorrow, it would all begin again.

***

For more information on this author, visit:
instagram.com/authortcmorgan

WAYWARD CORONA
BRIAN PAONE

The car bounced over the dusty hill into the darkness of the unlit, unpaved roadway, and the passenger instinctively reached for the oh-shit handle above his head. "Slow down, man. Where's the fire?"

"I just wanna take a look at her grave and make it back before someone catches us out here. I'm already on Gunny's last nerve."

"It's not even midnight yet," Corporal Mizzell answered, pointing to the car's dashboard clock. "No one's gonna even know we're missing for at least another hour."

"Is that it there?" Corporal Ross asked.

"All I know is that it's supposed to be behind a chain-link fence on the left-hand side, just beyond the tree line."

Ross pulled the car to the side of the road and activated his Maglite. He slowly scanned left to right, the beam infiltrated with floating pollen and small gnats.

"Over there. I see the fence."

Mizzell squinted. "I think I see the top of her tombstone too."

Ross turned off the car, secured his cover on his head, and stepped into the soft hush of silence, dotted only with the occasional chirp of some unknown insect in the woods.

When Mizzell slammed his passenger door, the chirping stopped. The two flashlight beams sliced through the surrounding blackness.

"She's really been seen traveling over the flight line, looking for her children?" Ross asked.

Mizzell cleared the front of the car, adjusted his cover so the brim wasn't obstructing his vertical sight, and the two marines took much smaller than normal steps toward the gate leading to the small graveyard.

"That's what all the stories say. Even an account of a pilot refusing to land one night because he said a woman was on the runway. The tower made him circle again so they could investigate. No one was out there."

The gravel under their boots cracked and popped with each step, and Ross placed his hand on the gate and pointed across the flight line in the distance.

"Why would they move her children's graves and leave her here?"

"I dunno, man," Mizzell said. "I don't even know when they did it. I was told they didn't realize they were her children when they relocated them."

"I heard they had to move all the graves from here to make room for the flight line. Doesn't make sense they would just leave *hers* here."

Ross swung open the gate, and they entered the small rectangular area, adorned by a single, crooked tombstone. The two marines traipsed toward the center, snapping dead grass and scattered twigs under their soles.

Mizzell raised his flashlight. "*Kissie Sykes. Age forty years.* Really? That's all they could think to put on her tombstone? No birth date? No death date?"

"No reason for her death?" Ross added. "Shit, she could've died two hundred years ago or fifty years ago for all we know."

"It's so creepy how her headstone leans to one side too. Like they either tried to move her with the other graves or—"

"Or she tried to escape herself."

"That's not funny, dude," Mizzell said and shone his flashlight over the top of her marker and into the far blackness of the flight line, elongating the headstone's shadow across the small fenced-in area.

"Look. You can see where her kids used to be."

Mizzell lowered his flashlight and saw four small rectangular divots in the dead grass near Kissie's grave.

"I'd say those are child size all right," Ross said.

Mizzell stepped left to investigate the two semi-filled holes on Kissie's right-hand side. Another pair were on her left. "Looks like they filled them in, but the earth has settled over the years."

"Think she'll ever find them? You know, her kids? Way over in Sunset Park where they were relocated?"

"Maybe she's not supposed to find them. Maybe this is her own private Purgatory."

"Morbid, dude. I wish we knew what she died of and how long she's been dead."

"Look it up. C'mon. Let's go back to the car. I'm gettin' eaten alive by these gnats," Mizzell said.

"Good to go," Ross agreed and turned toward his car, parked on the side of the dirt road.

The marines tossed their covers onto the dashboard, and Ross removed his phone from his camo shirt. Mizzell peered across the center console as Ross typed *Kissie Sykes haunting Cherry Point Marine Corps. Air Station* into the search field.

"Looks like it's just a lot of stories of people's personal sightings over the years," Ross said as he scrolled through the multiple links to related articles and websites. "Nothing about what year she died or how."

"Tons of pictures of her grave though," Mizzell added, quickly moving his gaze from Ross's phone to the faint outline of Kissie's leaning tombstone in the distance. "How far back do the stories—"

"Wait. There's a video."

Mizzell glanced at Ross's phone.

"It was posted earlier today," Ross said and tapped the Play button on his screen.

Mizzell nibbled on the corner of his index finger, peeling a small sliver of skin from underneath his fingernail as they watched the video follow two marines through the gate and into the small clearing, the sunlight dotting the screen with lens flares. The two marines stopped to inspect Kissie's headstone, and whoever was filming also stopped just behind them.

"Is your sound up?" Mizzell asked.

Ross pressed the Volume knob. "Yeah, man, it's all the way up."

"Sucks there's no sound."

Mizzell and Ross watched the backs of the marines' heads as one pointed across the flight line in the direction of Sunset Park, where Kissie's children were rumored to have been reburied. The other marine pointed to two of the small vacant grave-divots on the right.

"Do you know either of those douchebags?" Mizzell asked.

Ross shook his head.

The wind rocked the car, and Ross looked out his driver's side window. He couldn't see past his own reflection in the glass from the phone's backlight flooding the inside of the car.

"I'm ready to get out of here. The darkness is creeping me out, and I can't see her tomb—"

"*Shh!* Just one more second. The video's almost over," Mizzell said.

"It's not like we're gonna find out what we want to know from this video. It's just two stupid marines from earlier today."

"I'm not ... so sure of that."

Ross focused on his phone again and screamed. Mizzell yelled as Ross threw his phone across the center console, landing on the passenger floorboard next to Mizzell's boots, the screen facing upward.

The phone's upside-down video of two marines turning from Kissie Sykes's grave and approaching the car illuminated their faces. Then the screen went black.

Mizzell turned to Ross. "We gotta get the fuck out of here! That was *us*. Why was there sunlight in the video, and why the fuck didn't we know someone was following—?"

Ross swallowed hard, frozen to his seat, and didn't have the courage to ask Mizzell why he didn't finish his sentence. Even though he *knew* why Mizzell didn't finish his sentence.

When Mizzell's eyes grew wide but remained locked on Ross's face, Ross knew Mizzell had also smelled the putrid stench of rot and decay coming from the backseat, knew he had also felt the hot breath skimming along his neck, knew he had also heard the wheezing sound of air escaping struggling lungs, knew he had also seen the decomposed finger touching his cheek.

Mizzell screamed again, and Ross never remembered hearing him stop.

***

For more information on this author, visit: BrianPaone.com

UGLY GIRL
JASON PERE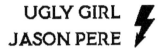

I hated her. She was an ugly girl with no friends and no money—
a pitiful overweight tragedy. We all gawked at the secondhand
rags she was forced to wear. She always sat by herself in class or at
lunch. Every day after second period, she snuck to the bathroom
to cry.

I indulged myself with something I'd wanted to do for years.
When I had her alone in the bathroom, I let my fists fly and
punched the ugly girl.

Then I felt the blood trickle down my knuckles as I pulled
my hands back from the broken mirror.

***

For more information on this author, visit:
amazon.com/author/jasonpere

LIKE HE'S SEEN A GHOST
MICHELLE PERRY

The first time our eyes met, I knew he was the one.

Bastard.

O'Keefe gaped at me from his driveway, the letter in his hand forgotten. I stood across the highway from his mailbox, staring.

He blanched, swayed on his feet, then ran back inside. A semi passed, and I used the cover to run too—through the forest, back to where I'd parked my car a quarter mile away in a McDonald's parking lot. I grabbed a bag out of the backseat and went inside the restroom to change clothes. My mother would have a heart attack if she saw me like this.

My reflection stopped me. With my hair up like this, sans makeup and in these clothes, I looked more like my twin Katie than myself. We both were members of the Lady Pioneerettes dance squad, so I had the same t-shirt and had found the same kind of running shoes and shorts to replicate what she was wearing that day—the day she was raped and murdered by Robert James O'Keefe on the trail she jogged every day.

Katie's boyfriend, Spencer, had given me the idea. We'd been sitting in the cafeteria when he'd started crying. As he wiped his tears, he said, "I can't wait until he goes to trial. Nikki, you should wear your hair up and just glare at him. He'd think he was seeing a ghost."

Seeing a ghost.

Turned out, that was how Spencer felt when he looked at me too. We'd been friends since kindergarten, but he couldn't deal with seeing me every day, so he began to avoid me. I understood. My own parents didn't look at me much anymore.

My face was a constant reminder of what we'd all lost.

The case against O'Keefe looked strong at first. DNA obtained from him matched the DNA recovered from Katie's body. But then he hired a new lawyer who got that thrown out, saying the police failed to give informed consent and explain the consequences of giving a sample. The DA said he couldn't take it to trial without more evidence. So, O'Keefe walked, and I came up with my own plan to get justice.

We attended a small high school, and my teachers were sympathetic. After that day, I developed a routine. I would start crying in class, and the teacher would send me to the guidance counselor's office. I'd talk to Mrs. Givens about Katie, then beg her not to call my parents. It was my senior year, and my schedule was pretty loose anyway, so she'd tell me to take a walk around the building and collect myself.

I'd take a walk, alright—straight to my car in the parking lot and then somewhere to change clothes and find O'Keefe. I wore the same outfit every time, and it began to feel like a superhero outfit.

He worked a dead-end job at Gino's Pizza in the food court at the mall. I'd go stand by the Smoothie King and stare until he'd look up and notice me.

I'd spent weeks studying his schedule. I knew what time he'd clock out and what bus he'd take home. I never showed any sign of the seething rage I felt. I kept my face blank, but never stopped staring. I'd follow him anywhere I could, anywhere I felt safe in a crowd.

It was working, I thought. He began to lose weight, to look pale and hunted. He stopped leaving the house except to go to work, and he eventually stopped doing that.

I fantasized about him breaking down and confessing to the police, but that wasn't how it played out.

One day, I stood outside his house in my usual spot. The

cold air nipped at my bare legs, but I didn't care. I felt he was close to breaking, and I was right. Movement of his curtains drew my attention, then the front door swung open.

"Leave me alone!" he bellowed and charged from the house, brandishing a baseball bat.

My heart leapt, and I sprinted to the woods. A horn blared behind me, brakes squealed, and there was an awful thunking sound. I dared to look around. O'Keefe lay on the side of the road. An older lady jumped out of the flower van she'd hit him with and ran towards him, shrieking. When I saw he wasn't getting up, I jogged over to them.

His eyes widened when he saw me, and he started begging, "No, no. No! Please!"

"Call nine-one-one!" I told her, and when she turned away to do it, I grinned at him, inspiring a new wave of frantic babbling.

"I'm sorry!" he gasped.

"Sorry for what?" I hissed. "Say it."

"I'm sorry I hurt you. I'm sorry I killed you."

I made a tsking sound. "You're losing a lot of blood. I don't think you're going to make it."

I didn't have much time. For the old lady's benefit, I screamed, "I don't think he's breathing!"

That inspired another burst of chatter to the operator. Careful to use my body to block her view, I used the tail of my Pioneerette shirt to make sure he wasn't. The last face my sister saw was his, and in a way, the last face he saw was hers.

Kind of poetic, I thought.

Other people were stopping to help now. I stood and backed away from him, then went to pat the old lady's shoulder. People pushed past us to check his pulse.

The old lady didn't seem to notice me at all. She was still screaming at the dispatcher. I slipped away.

Before my parents came home that day, I burned my outfit in the firepit, taking satisfaction that this time it was his blood, not hers, soaking the Pioneerettes shirt.

I read the papers, watched the news coverage for any mention of a blonde jogger at the scene, but there was nothing. I practiced my blank stare in case the police questioned me.

They never did.

I was at school that day, anyway, according to records.

FATAL APPLICATION
K. A. RIEDER

Sandra lay in bed scrolling through the apps on her phone. Her mouth curved into a smile as she imagined what her friends would say. "What are you doing spending your Friday night alone in bed, playing Candy Crush? It's been years since your divorce. It's time to get out there again."

Something caught her eye. An app she hadn't seen before. It was a black icon with a red question mark. Sandra tapped on the app. Nothing happened. She attempted to delete the app, but it wouldn't do that either. Deciding to look at it more tomorrow, Sandra put her phone back on the nightstand and rolled over to sleep.

Sandra woke to a loud beep. Startled, she rolled over to look at the clock. 11:12 p.m. The beeping started again, and her phone lit up. Rubbing her weary eyes, she glanced at the screen. It was an alert from the unknown app. Tapping open, she stared at the screen and couldn't help but smile as a message flashed on the screen.

Challenge 1: Go to a bar, and buy a man a drink.

Two icons showed under the message, Accept and Decline. Sandra shook her head as she tapped Decline. One of her friends must have created the app to try and get her to go out. Another beep. She looked at the new alert.

Are you sure you don't want to reconsider?

They were persistent, she would give them that. Sandra tapped Decline again. Beep! Starting to get frustrated now, she tapped on the alert.

Maybe I am not being clear enough.

Sandra began to feel nervous. It didn't sound like her friends anymore. They'd always encouraged her to get out, but they had never been forceful like this. Convincing herself she was being paranoid, she swallowed the lump in her throat and hit Decline. She sat, staring at the phone, hoping another alert would not appear.

Beep!

Trying to slow her racing heart, Sandra tapped on the alert.

Clearly, you need some convincing.

A video appeared before her. Sandra's heart leapt into her mouth, and her pulse raced. There, in the middle of the screen, was her twenty-one-year-old daughter, Mikayla. Bound to a chair, her head pulled back by her ponytail, and a large knife held to her throat by someone dressed in a ski mask. The video disappeared, and a message took its place.

It's simple. To save your daughter, you must complete the challenges. Fail, your daughter dies. Call the police, your daughter dies. Alert anyone at all and it's game over! Accept or decline?

A feeling of nausea washed over Sandra as she hit Accept. A new alert appeared on the screen.

In your wardrobe, you will find a red dress. Wear it. Make yourself look pretty. Makeup, hair, the works. Go to Maginty's bar and look for the man sitting alone. He will be wearing a suit with a red tie. Sit next to him, and buy him a drink.

The message was replaced with a large timer. Thirty minutes. She didn't have time to think as the numbers on her phone began to count down. Rushing to her wardrobe, she found the red dress. It wasn't hers. She wrestled with her fear as she tried to wipe all thoughts of a stranger creeping into her house and hanging the dress there. She slid on the dress, threw her hair into a bun, and willed her hand to stop shaking as she applied her lipstick.

The timer was down to sixty seconds by the time she made it to the bar. She spotted the man and sat next to him. "Can I buy you a drink?"

The man looked at the plunging neckline of her dress and smiled.

Beep!

Challenge completed. Challenge 2: Taped to the underside of your stool, you will find a hotel key. Take him up to Room 12.

Sandra looked frantically around the room for someone watching her but couldn't see anyone. She tapped Accept. Her heart pounded as she reached beneath the stool and felt the keys. The timer was back. Ten minutes. Steadying her breath, Sandra smiled seductively and waved the room key at the suited man.

There were still three minutes left on the timer when she entered Room 12 with the man from the bar.

Challenge completed. Challenge 3: Screw him. But remember, alert him and your daughter dies.

Sliding her dress down off her shoulders, she pushed the man onto the bed. He had his pants off in a second. Her skin crawled and her stomach lurched as she straddled the stranger. An image of her daughter with a knife to her throat swam through her mind. Gritting her teeth, she lowered herself onto the man, closed her eyes, and prayed it would all be over soon.

The man grunted as he thrust into her one last time. The sound made Sandra want to vomit, but she held it down. Rolling off him, she reached out for her phone again as the man threw a rolled-up wad of cash onto the bed next to her and made his way to the shower.

Beep!

Challenge completed. Challenge 4: Open the bedside drawer. You're going to need what's in there.

Fear flooded Sandra's body as she reached into the draw and her fingers curled over something cold and metallic. She stared, horrified at the gun gripped between her fingers.

Beep.

You know what to do.

There was no way she could kill someone. Her head bowed as she thought of Mikayla. "I'm sorry," she whispered as she tapped Decline.

Are you sure?

Angry now that some stranger had turned her into a prostitute and was now trying to force her to become a murderer, Sandra jabbed the decline icon. She would save Mikayla another way.

Beep.

Sandra's resolve faltered as she opened the alert. She watched, horrified as the man in the ski mask pulled out a pair of pruning shears, held them around the base of Mikayla's index finger, and clamped shut. Sandra fell to the ground, vomit erupting violently from her as the sound of Mikayla's screams filled the room.

Beep.

Accept or decline?

Sandra lifted her shaking finger to the screen and tapped Accept. A timer appeared. Two minutes. With shaking legs, she stood slowly and grabbed the gun. Her knees threatened to collapse as she walked towards the bathroom, the sound of running water not quite drowning out the pounding in her ears.

The water stopped as she entered the room, and the man pulled back the curtain. His smile faded as he registered the scene in front of him. Sandra stood, hands shaking uncontrollably, the gun held up between herself and the man.

"What the hell are you doing?" the man yelled. "Do you want more money? Take it!"

Sandra stood, unable to move as the man stared at her in horror, begging for his life.

Beep!

You're running out of time. Maybe you need more

motivation.

Sandra watched as the man in the ski mask removed another of Mikayla's fingers.

The counter on her phone began to beep. *10 ... 9 ... 8 ...*

"I'm sorry." A tear slid down her cheek as she pulled the trigger. Sandra's ears rang as the sound from the gun echoed around the tiled bathroom. She watched as the man slid down the shower, leaving a trail of blood on the wall behind him. There was no way the gunshot had gone unheard.

Grabbing her phone, Sandra raced out to the street. Stumbling to the gutter, Sandra's stomach heaved again as bile splashed onto the curb. Fumbling for her phone, she waited, heart pounding, pulse racing.

Beep.

An address appeared on the screen, and Sandra sped off in her car, calling the police on the way.

Sandra arrived at the abandoned warehouse and rushed to Mikayla, who was sitting alone, still bound to the chair. As the sound of sirens filled the air, Sandra hurried to untie her daughter's mutilated hands. Within minutes, the warehouse was surrounded by police, but it was too late. The sadistic animal that had tortured her daughter was gone.

As the ambulance officers loaded Mikayla onto a gurney, Sandra told the police everything, including the murder of the suited man at the hotel. Sandra was cuffed and put into the back of a cop car as she watched Mikayla get loaded into the ambulance.

Inside the ambulance, the officer sitting in the back with Mikayla pulled out her phone and showed it to the driver. "Any idea what this is? It won't open."

As Mikayla glanced over, she saw a black icon with a red question mark, and a blood curdling scream escaped her.

"She's having a meltdown," the ambulance officer called as

she pushed a long needle containing a sedative into Mikayla's arm.

Drowsiness overtook Mikayla, and her body relaxed as the ambulance doors shut. But even through the fogginess, she heard the unmistakable beep of a phone receiving an alert.

***

For more information on this author, visit:
facebook.com/author.k.a.rieder

THE VILE VERMIN OF WALSH
CHRIS RULAND

Nick stepped off his porch and looked at his watch. It was just after eight p.m., meaning that the sun would be setting soon. *That's okay,* he thought. *Just a quick jog down a country road.* Besides, nothing ever happened out here in the sleepy country town of Walsh after eight o'clock.

He put his hands on his hips and took in a deep breath, his chest rising with hubris as he felt a renewed sense of hope. Even though his soon-to-be ex-wife had deprived him of health insurance, he had found other ways to get his health needs under control. The last thing that his therapist had told him before Nick's bank account had dwindled, leaving him without the funds to go to therapy anymore, was to get some exercise, and the prospect of an easy jog down a country road seemed to be exactly the thing that could lift his spirit.

And although he couldn't afford the antidepressants anymore, he had found a kid in town who sold him the very same drug for only twenty bucks a week. "This is gonna be so much better than the stuff your doctor gave you," the kid had said. That would do for now, at least until Nick could find a better job. He had swallowed one of those little white pills just before heading out the door for his jog, and he felt good. He felt oh-so-good.

He rounded the bend to Webster Road and headed down the long, hilly road that was covered in a canopy of ancient oak trees. The sun was low enough in the horizon that he was in absolute shade and the cool, spring air felt refreshing. Nick jogged steadily but took some walking breaks. He was out of shape, but that wasn't going to stop him from starting a productive exercise routine.

Nick glanced at his phone, the Watch Me Run app telling him he had gone a whole mile in just under ten minutes. His ankles burned, and his heart raced, but he felt *good*. He decided that another mile down the road would not be a problem. He would be getting back to his home just as it got dark, and he'd have plenty of time for a relaxing shower and maybe a couple of beers.

When Nick looked up from his phone, he saw an old, wrinkled face in the trunk of one of the oak trees. It was looking right at him. "Turn back," it said in a gravelly voice. "You're going to get tired."

Nick laughed. "How would you know? Have you ever run before?"

The old tree scrunched its eyebrows, shooting a look of irritation back at Nick. "Don't say I didn't warn you. And watch out for the squirrels."

Nick raised an eyebrow. He hadn't considered the squirrels. He looked up and saw one bounding along the old tree's branch, which hung over the road directly over Nick's head. It froze and looked down at him, its cheeks bulging with nuts, its tail flicking. It spat out the nuts and made an awful squeaking noise, then raised up on its hind legs and put its hands to its mouth, letting out a vile screech that echoed in the depths of the forest. Then it looked down at Nick, its eyes glowing red. "We're coming for you," it said in an unnaturally deep voice.

Nick laughed. "Shut your mouth!" he yelled and kept running. A squirrel and a tree weren't going to ruin his run.

He nearly collapsed when he got to the two-mile mark. Looking at the timer on his phone, Nick realized that the second mile had taken nearly twice as long to run as the first mile. The sun had sunk so low that it was almost night. There were no lights out here in the country, other than the occasional car passing by, of which he had only seen one this entire time.

He turned back and started to walk home. He had wanted to be back before nightfall but that was no longer possible. He tried walking at a brisk pace but even that was painful.

He froze when he realized that he could hear each and every tree in the forest calling out to him. He covered his ears with his palms and shook his head, but he looked in all directions and saw old, wrinkled faces in each of the tree trunks, and their mouths were all moving, repeating the same words: "The squirrels. The squirrels."

"Knock it off!" he shouted over the rhythmic chanting and kept walking as fast as he could. But then he heard another sound. It was like the screeching that the squirrel on the old oak tree had made, only this was a chorus of at least a hundred squirrel voices. It created a deafening echo that reverberated throughout the forest. He turned back and saw several hundred, maybe several thousand squirrels in rank and file in the road behind him. They were following him, their tails bouncing fluidly with their movements. As Nick stopped, so did they.

Nick turned and started running, though he felt so tired he wanted to vomit. Half-turning, he saw the squirrels behind him begin to follow, a sea of red and brown fur reciprocating his movements like tiny waves, a hoard of indiscernible vermin trailing him like obedient dogs following their master.

"Shoo!" he yelled, but they continued unabated. He ran faster, every muscle burning. Turning back, he saw the squirrels quicken their pace. "Get!" he shouted. "Leave me alone!"

But the squirrels only followed faster.

Nick was sprinting when his legs gave out. He stumbled to the earth and smacked his head on the ground before spewing a fountain of vomit and laying his head in it. Lacking any individuality, the squirrels erupted in a chorus of chatter.

They surrounded him and froze.

One squirrel stepped out from the hoard. Nick knew that it

was the same one he had seen on the old oak tree. "Why are you doing this?" Nick gurgled, vomit dripping from his lips.

"You have been chosen," it said.

"I don't want to be chosen! I want to go home!"

"It's too late," it answered. "What's done is done."

Nick screamed as the squirrels closed in on him, fangs dripping with a yellow slime, eyes glowing red. The massive hoard leapt upon him in a voracious, carnivorous frenzy, and his screams were quickly dampened like a smothered candle flame.

"Very strange," the medical examiner said, looking at her computer monitor. "Very strange, indeed."

The fat, balding detective looked up from his notepad. "What's strange?" he asked.

The medical examiner leaned forward and looked at the detective over the rim of her glasses. "You said that the deputies found him covered in bite wounds, like he had been gnawed upon?"

"Yes. It was very clear to everyone who saw the corpse that he'd been eaten alive. Do your findings show any different?"

"No, that isn't it. That is *exactly* what my findings show. But it appears, without any doubt in my mind, that all of the wounds were self-inflicted."

"You mean he killed himself first?"

"No, Detective. I mean that he ate his own flesh until he bled to death. The bite marks, the abrasions, he did all of it to himself."

"How is that possible?"

"I've heard of rare cases of this happening. The cause of death was exsanguination—massive blood loss—to a degree I've never seen before. He lost nearly four liters of blood. That's almost eighty percent of his blood supply."

The detective grunted. "So now the question is, why?"

"His bloodwork showed that he had high concentrations of lysergic acid diethylamide."

The detective turned his head with curiosity. "He was high on acid?"

"Yes," she replied. "He must have taken a large dose of LSD right before he went out jogging."

"Well, that tells us just about everything we need to know. I guess we can close this case. Now we have to find out where he got the drugs. Thanks for all of your help, Doctor."

The detective left the office, though he still sensed a lack of closure. He thought about the crime scene, how little blood was actually there on the dirt road. Where had it all gone?

He drove his car out of the county office lot, and instead of returning home, he decided to head back to the crime scene.

When he arrived, he parked his car next to the spot where the body had been found, and he got out and looked around and at the road. Then he looked up, and he saw a squirrel on the tree branch of an old oak tree above his head. It flicked its tail and stared with red eyes.

The detective locked eyes with the animal as it let out an awful, vile screech.

***

For more information on this author, visit:
@cmruland — Twitter

THE INTERVIEW
JARED SIZEMORE ⚡

Dale was so nervous about the job interview he didn't notice the police investigation in the rear of the building. Dale sat in his white Ford Explorer outside of Martin & Coons—one of the top financial planning firms in the city—going over his notes one last time, making sure he was ready to nail this interview. After ten other companies had turned him down, this was his last good chance. Dale had promised his wife, Molly, and his unborn daughter that he would find a job soon. Each night he whispered to his daughter—nine months along—and figured if he made a promise to her, he would work harder to keep it. He jammed his notes back into his folder, straightened up his tie, and bounded toward the main entrance.

Portfolio in hand, Dale swept in the lobby door and smiled widely at the receptionist, who appeared to be right out of the 1940s. She had curly black but greying hair and wore a white, button-up blouse with a small collar and puffy sleeves.

Dale tried to make eye contact, but her head was hunched down a bit over some papers on her desk. "Hi, I'm Dale Harris. I'm here to interview for the financial advisor position. I was supposed to ask for John."

Her gaze rose up slowly to meet his, revealing her pale skin and dark eyes. "Yeesss," she said with a grating, whispery voice. "John no longer works here." She stamped down hard with an old-fashioned rubber stamper. *Plunk.*

"Oh, really?" said Dale. "I hadn't heard that. Is there someone else I should see?"

She picked up a vintage silver letter opener, shaped like a sword, and pointed down the hallway. Waiting for her to speak but getting nothing, Dale just headed in the direction she pointed.

Plunk. She kept stamping with that stamper as if she was plugging holes in the *Titanic*'s deck. Dale made his way down the hallway, unsure where to go. He passed a room where a few people were gathered and speaking in hushed voices. He tried not to stare inside but ... Were women crying in there? Someone shut the door. Dale stood awkwardly by a copy machine and waited.

After a minute, an older, balding man approached. "Can I help you?"

Dale smiled. "I'm here to interview for the financial advisor position. I was told to head this way."

"Oh, right. I'm so sorry, but today is not the best day. Can you come back tomorrow?"

Dale, disappointed, faked his response. "Sure! Absolutely. Should I ask for you?"

"Yes, that will be fine. I'm Art, one of the managers here." Art shook Dale's hand.

"Dale Harris, great to meet you."

"See you tomorrow, Dale. And again, I apologize. Nine a.m. good?"

"Perfect. See you then."

The next morning, Dale showed up in the lobby at 8:45 a.m. The receptionist was still pounding that stamper. *Plunk.*

He flashed his smile. "Good morning! I'm here to see Art for an interview."

Her gaze rose to meet his. "Yeesss, Art no longer works here," said the whispery, grating voice.

Dale's eyes went wide. Was this a joke? The universe did not want him to find a job. His career was becoming a joke, but he couldn't let his family down by blowing this. "Okay. Should I—"

The receptionist picked up the letter opener and pointed down the hallway.

Dale nodded and marched down the hallway. He reached the same spot by the copy machine as the day before but saw no one in the office. That is until a well-groomed man in a tailored grey suit approached. "Dale, right?"

"Yes!" said Dale, smiling.

"I'm Bill Martin, the CEO here. Let's go to my office." Bill took Dale's hand and crushed it in a too-firm handshake.

Dale followed Bill into his spacious corner office and at Bill's directive, took a seat in a comfortable plush leather chair that squeaked as he slid into it. Dale guessed Bill to be in his early sixties but in great shape and still had most of his hair. Old football trophies lined a trophy case on the wall.

Bill sat behind his enormous, neatly organized desk. "I apologize for the strangeness, Dale, but this has been a very rough week for our company, as you probably know."

Dale strained to show his poker face. He felt stupid for having no idea what Bill was talking about. One of the first rules of interviewing was to do your research about the company. He didn't know how to answer—lie and pretend he knew or admit ignorance and lose the job?

Mercifully, Bill continued. "Did you see it on the news?"

The news? Dale shook his head. "Actually, no. I've been pretty busy prepping for this. On Sunday, my wife had a false alarm with the baby, so we spent six hours at the hospital. Then I watched the game last night. I notice you're a football fan too. More than a fan."

Bill ignored Dale's attempt at connecting on common interests. "Well, it's hard to say it, so I'll just say it. We've had two people in our office … murdered this week."

"Murdered?" blurted Dale. That did explain the odd atmosphere.

Bill nodded. A tear went down his cheek. He wiped it away. "Art was a friend of mine, an old friend."

"Art? I just met him yesterday!"

Bill exhaled. "Yes, indeed. The office is closed today for the investigation, but I came in by myself to take care of some odds and ends. And I really wanted to meet with you since Art told me you were coming back today. He and I went to school together. He raised three wonderful children. Anyway, sorry, Dale. This is straying off the purpose of an interview. Tell me more about yourself and why you would be a good fit to work here."

Dale launched into his rehearsed spiel about his experience, credentials, and the value he would bring to the company. His education was impeccable. Bill seemed to be impressed. Bill explained a little about the company's history and how his grandfather started it after the Second World War. He then asked Dale specific questions about the industry, which Dale fielded brilliantly. After about thirty minutes, Bill politely got up and made a phone call.

Dale waited nervously in the comfy chair, taking the chance to look over his notes and jot down a few more. He put his hand on his knee to keep it from shaking. And he really had to pee.

Bill returned. "Well, Dale, I can't give official confirmation just yet, but everything looks great. You should be hearing from us very soon. I think you'll have a bright future here."

"Thank you so much, Mr. Martin."

"Call me Bill."

Bill walked Dale down the hallway toward the main entrance.

"Bill, is there a men's room on the way out?" asked Dale. "Never mind, I'll just ask the receptionist."

Bill cocked his head. "We don't have a receptionist."

Dale felt stupid again. "Uh … yes you … I've spoken to her each time I've come here. She's always stamping that thing."

Bill looked puzzled. "Hmm. We had one in the summer, but she quit. A young gal, college student."

"It was an older lady. Middle-aged," said Dale.

"Maybe you spoke to the cleaning lady. What did she look like?"

"Black, greying hair. A blouse I swear was from the 1940s."

"Interesting," said Bill. "That reminds me. My grandfather told me about a receptionist here back in the early days who had a mental breakdown. She went truly crazy. She threatened him once, and he finally had her committed to a mental hospital. I heard she committed suicide there. Anyway, just an old ghost story. Take care, Dale." He motioned toward the lobby.

No one sat at the front desk.

Dale inched past the desk as if it was a landmine that could explode any second. He rushed out the door, jumped in his car, and headed home.

That night, Dale decided not to tell Molly about the murders or any of the other weirdness; it might send her into false labor again.

The nightly news was on while they were eating a spaghetti dinner together. Molly was asking Dale about cloth versus regular diapers when the female news anchor's breaking report grabbed Dale's attention: "*CEO Bill Martin of the Martin & Coons financial planning firm was found dead this afternoon in the rear of the company's building. Apparently, he was stabbed in the back with a letter opener. This happened even despite the ongoing police presence from the week's previous murders. No suspect has yet been found.*"

Dale dropped his meatball on the floor. He stared speechless at the TV for a full minute until Molly said, "Honey, your phone is vibrating!"

She handed him the phone. The caller ID indicated: *Martin & Coons.*

Shaking, Dale pushed the answer button. "Hello?"

"Yeesss, can you start tomorrow?" said the receptionist.

***

For more information on this author, visit: jaredsizemore.com

RECOGNITION
ERIN SKOLNEY ⚡

On the morning of his big presentation, Craig Moyer woke up with a headache. He stood from his bed, and the pain shot across his temple, hot and sharp.

Not today, he thought, and he swallowed two ibuprofens. His presentation was too important for his mind to be clouded by pain. He decided to swallow an extra ibuprofen, just in case.

Then, he set about getting ready. He had set his alarm to wake him up early, so he would have plenty of time to prepare. He brushed his teeth and combed his dark hair, taking extra care to tame the cowlick over his left eye. His hair had started graying recently, a few light flecks making their appearance. He had almost dyed his hair to cover the signs of aging, but his secretary, Trish, had told him it looked distinguished. He was sleeping with her, and she liked it, so he kept his hair as it was. She may have been right though, because he'd noticed people had treated him with greater respect over the past month. Maybe it was the graying hair, maybe not, but he enjoyed the authority he seemed to command of late.

Craig trimmed his short beard and then slipped the clear contact lenses over his blue-gray eyes. Today he became the face of the company. Determined to represent them well, he chose his best suit and made sure everything down to the pocket square looked perfectly in place before he stepped out the door of his apartment.

A biting wind ripped through him, but it was a short walk to the office. He had left his apartment early, with enough time to stop at the coffee shop on the corner. Caffeine would keep him awake and alert and possibly also combat his headache.

It hadn't dulled.

Craig stepped inside and breathed in the rich aroma of coffee and fresh-baked pastries. The cafe was mostly empty except for a man in the corner, back turned to him, newspaper open in his lap. It was too early even for the morning rush.

Craig always ordered the same drink, and so he didn't need any time to look at the menu. His phone buzzed as he approached the counter. He fished it from his suit pocket to check the alert while he ordered.

"Caramel macchiato, skim milk, no whip," he said as he read the email that had arrived: reminders about the presentation.

"One mocha coming up," the barista replied.

"No," Craig said, looking up from his phone.

The barista turned, and Craig forgot what he had been about to say. He stared into the same blue-grey eyes he had just seen in the bathroom mirror. The barista had the same neatly-trimmed beard. His hair was smoothed back, identical to Craig's, with the same cowlick barely pulling outward from where it had been combed down. Craig was looking in a mirror—except when he raised a hand to smooth down his hair, the mirror-image barista only looked at him, waiting for clarification.

Craig shook his head. "One mocha," he found himself saying. He didn't know where the words had come from, but no other words formed in his mind.

He watched himself—no, the barista—prepare the beverage. His headache intensified. With the barista's back to him, Craig felt certain the headache had caused the earlier familiarity. His shoulders were broader than the barista's. And he stood straighter, didn't he? He was certain he was a couple of inches taller. It had to have been an illusion. A trick of his mind. Yet when the barista handed him his mocha—not his usual order—Craig once again looked into his own face.

In fact, as the barista turned toward the espresso machine,

Craig noticed a small pink scar just below the left side of the barista's jaw. His fingers touched his own scar, the small raised triangle where he'd fallen and stabbed his chin on a tree branch while riding his bike as a child.

Craig set down the coffee and left in a daze.

As he opened the door, he took one last look at the barista and nearly bumped into the man entering.

"Excuse me," Craig said, then stopped and stared at the man in disbelief.

Dark hair. Blue-gray eyes. A perfectly trimmed beard.

"Can I help you?" the man asked.

Craig couldn't speak. He felt dizzy. He managed to divert his gaze and stumble into the crisp morning. He sucked in air and forced his feet to walk toward the office. He had a presentation to give. He tried to recite his talking points, but he kept thinking about the two men in the coffee shop.

God, his head hurt. The pain was a knife.

Craig passed a woman with her two kids, and he smiled and waved. But when they smiled and waved back, he felt his stomach drop and his blood run cold. His skin grew clammy, his breathing shallow. He recognized them all. They may as well have stepped right out of the photograph taken twenty years earlier. Him, with his unruly curls. His younger brother, lighter-haired and freckled. His mom with the warm smile he'd thought of every day since she had died two years ago.

He stumbled backward and bumped into a man.

"I'm so sorry," Craig said, once again meeting his own gaze.

Craig's head pounded, and he rubbed his temple with both hands.

He looked down the street. A handful of people strode down the sidewalk. Men. All the same height. Same build. Same hair. He knew the rest.

Craig couldn't hear over the hammering in his head. His

thoughts were dizzying. He needed to sit. No, he needed to move.

He kept walking. He didn't know which direction he was headed. Vaguely he remembered he had somewhere to go.

A man with a briefcase in one hand and a coffee in the other appeared to look around frantically before bumping into him. The man steadied himself and met his gaze. He looked into the man's blue-gray eyes. He wished his eyes were that same haunting shade.

"I'm so sorry," the man said. "I'm having a very strange morning. I have a presentation at work, and I have the worst headache!"

"Don't worry about it," he said.

The man kept walking in one direction, and Craig walked in the other. More people passed him.

He recognized no one.

***

For more information on this author, visit:
facebook.com/SkolneyWrites

THE QUEEN'S MASSACRE
MIKA SPRUILL

The queen sat upon her throne, awaiting her army's return. She was anxious when her soldiers were away—especially Bennett. The whole lot of them were boisterous and wild, but she had grown fond of their antics. She hated when they left the colony outside of her control, even if she knew Bennet would keep them in line. These were her best warriors yet. They'd fought off invaders, predators, and even rebels from within their own walls. They were due back soon, but with every passing hour, the queen grew more agitated. Her kingdom had grown so quickly that new enemies lurked around every corner. She needed her army.

It was almost a week ago that her soldiers had set out for new lands in search of territory and food. Though days had passed without word, the squire had come that very morning to announce that a bounty was on its return. Upon his declaration, the queen ordered him out.

"Away! Gather everyone in the Common Hall at once. Let us be ready to reap our rewards." And with haste, it was done. Servants were mustered from every corner of the palace. The queen's attendants helped her from her bed, and there in the Common Hall, they all waited.

Excited chatter filled the massive room, but the queen was too tired to silence them. Her ironhanded rule was softened by her delicate condition. She was pregnant again—her tenth, though this was far from her last. A queen's duty was to control the bloodlines, even at the expense of her own body. It was an ancestral burden she bore with honor, but at the moment, she felt hot and fat. The air was too warm for comfort. She'd almost given up, sent everyone out, and waddled back to her bed when the first of her soldiers burst into the room, weighed down with goods. She watched them file in anxiously, checking each face until she saw him. Bennett was the last in line.

An excited rumble worked through the crowd as the soldiers presented their gifts to the queen.

"A nectar," Bennett explained of the offering.

The queen was overjoyed. "Delicious! Everyone must try this."

They tasted the syrupy concoction until every belly was content. Then the parade of supplies continued, and the entire colony was rewarded for their hard work with a buffet of delicacies.

When the queen asked for the soldier who discovered their new libation, it was Talia who stepped forward, stately and feminine. The queen hefted herself up to bestow her gratitude. Talia was shaking. Without warning, she fell before the queen's feet, spewing up all she had eaten.

"Someone remove her and see to her needs," the queen ordered, but each of her soldiers had taken to the same illness, shivering on the ground with contorted faces and vomiting the contents of their stomachs.

No one would help, no one approached. The smell of death swirled through the room as the dead soldiers lay prostrate before her.

To preserve the others, the queen ordered the room to be cleared at once, and everyone was sent home, but it was for naught. The remaining crowd was already afflicted and seized like lightning coursed their veins. They were dying, every last one of them.

The queen watched in horror as her own stomach curled, and she fought to steady her shaking hands. She was powerless; a frightening circumstance she was unprepared to handle. Through fading eyes, she looked out to her family, her servants and subjects, her sweet Bennet, and found only listless bodies, unresponsive to her calls. Then finally, stillness.

A peaceful lull.

Two voices broke through the silence, reverberating the walls of the Common Hall. They were deep, masculine voices that came from outside and spoke in foreign tongues the queen did not understand. She struggled to hear them, hoping for an answer.

"Howdy, Tom," said one. "You reckon I put out enough of that ant poison? Ain't no dead ants near it."

"Yup. See, it's all tasty to them little pests. They supposed to take it back to their nest for the rest of the colony to eat, even the queen. Then the poison kicks in, and they all die together. It's all real peaceful and such. That's how it works."

Tommy and Billy were simple country folk. They kicked dirt over the opening to the ant hill, unaware that the queen had gurgled her dying breath under their very feet.

***

For more information on this author, visit:
facebook.com/mikaspru

FOR THE WANT OF A NAME ⚡
DAWN TAYLOR

The boy was not more than seven years old, but he knew what he wanted and was determined to get it. He stopped at Clauncey's Hardware every day after school to make sure it was still there. His fingers smudged the glass display case as he surveyed the inventory he knew so well.

Yes. It was still there. The radio. His radio. The one he had been saving his allowance to buy. Only a few more weeks and it would belong to him. Mr. Clauncey would ring the purchase on his massive cash register, place it in a brown paper bag, and the boy would claim his prize.

His father said he could buy it, but he had to pay for it. Each week, the boy removed the plastic lid from a dented Folger's can. He dumped his coins onto the bedroom's hardwood floor and created stacks of currency in appropriate denominations. Counting money was serious business.

He had saved six dollars and fifty-nine cents. The radio cost seven dollars and ninety-nine cents. He reached for the small pad and pencil stored in the can. Double checking his math, he calculated he needed one dollar and forty cents. Receiving his fifty-cent weekly allowance, his purchase was guaranteed in three weeks. Now he had to wait—the hardest part.

Mr. Clauncey smiled every afternoon when the boy entered the store. After a quick hello, the boy rushed to the display case. His enthusiasm amused the storeowner. Other boys sprinted to the sporting goods section to admire baseball bats or fishing poles. This boy was different somehow. This one was strong-minded, as if he were on a mission.

The radio the boy coveted was not anything special, just a

pocket-sized AM transistor model. The store sold two or three of them weekly. Mr. Clauncey reminded his clerks to restock the display case after ringing a sale. He did not want the boy disappointed to discover *his* radio had been sold.

On the Friday before spring break, the boy dashed through the door. He hurried to the display case to ensure the radio was in its place. Satisfied, he ran to the counter to find Mr. Clauncey unpacking a case of screwdrivers.

The boy swallowed hard to catch his breath. "I have my money. All of it. I'm buying the radio today."

"Then we best fetch it out of the case, if it's still there."

The boy watched Mr. Clauncey select a small key from several on his key ring. The store owner unlocked the case and laid the radio on the glass. The boy inspected it, running his hands over the smooth black plastic.

"Turn it on. Make sure it works."

The boy pressed a button and used his fingernail to turn the notched dial. His face gleamed as music replaced static. Mr. Clauncey secured the lock and motioned for his customer to the counter.

Mr. Clauncey slid the radio, complete with ear jack, into the manufacturer's box. "That's seven dollars, ninety-nine cents, plus fifty-six cents sales tax ... Brings the total to eight dollars and fifty-five cents, please."

The price appeared on the gigantic cash register as the till opened.

Tax? Nobody told me about that.

The boy reached into his coat pocket and withdrew a leather pouch. He had counted his stash five times last night. He knew it contained exactly eight dollars and nine cents. Heat crawled up his neck and reddened his face as he glanced at the register and back to his pouch. He had waited four months to claim his treasure—a lifetime for a poor kid.

"Don't have enough."

He turned his head so Mr. Clauncey would not see a big boy cry. He returned his pouch, along with his crushed dream, to his pocket.

Mr. Clauncey had grown fond of the youngster. He was different from the older boys who browsed the store. The others disorganized the aisles and vanished just as quickly. This boy would take time to chat. Some afternoons, he was the only company the old man had. The boy had proven his integrity; he had earned the radio.

"Well, tell you what. How 'bout paying me with the money you have now. And if you're willing, sweep the floor for the rest."

The boy wiped his nose with his shirt's hem. A glimmer of a smile returned. "Really?"

Mr. Clauncey nodded. "Grab that broom there, and we've got a deal."

The boy eyed the bag with the receipt stapled to it.

"Don't worry. It'll be there when you're finished."

Mr. Clauncey returned to unpacking the screwdrivers as he watched the boy maneuver the broom twice his size. The youngster methodically began at the rear of the store and swept a pile of dirt containing old price tags and bits of string to the left of the counter.

"Good enough, boy. I'll take it from here."

Mr. Clauncey exchanged the broom for the radio.

The grin that spread across the boy's freckled face had been priceless.

Mr. Clauncey recalled the boy's expression while he sat in his wheelchair in the dementia unit. Mr. Clauncey's confusion had caused him to misuse silverware at times and to fail to recognize his daughter during her visits. He spent his days at the window, gazing at nothing in particular as one day drifted into the next.

Clauncey's Hardware had closed after operating for forty-six years. Hundreds of people had shopped at his store. Mr. Clauncey had known most of his customers on a first-name basis. He had rung up countless purchases during those years, but he had never forgotten the boy buying the radio.

He chuckled as he realized he had never asked the boy's name. It had not seemed important all those years ago; it was not important now.

***

For more information on this author, visit: Dawnmtaylor.com

BARELY A STORY
WILLIAM THATCH

Sigh.

There she goes again. Screaming bloody murder. Just once, I wish when she came down the stairs in the morning, she wouldn't start screaming the second she saw me. I had a rough night too, y'know! No car. Cabs wouldn't stop for me. Public transit sped away. I had to walk hours to get here in the middle of the night. All I want is a nice, quiet breakfast; is that too much to ask?

She couldn't even bother to keep my usual stocked in the cupboard either. This isn't the first time we've gone through this, Carol! Jesus, why do you have to be such a bare-skinned bitch?

Alright, that's not fair. I'm tired and hungry and a little grumpy; the door was locked. I had to break the window on the door so that I could unlock it. Is it too much to just leave a jar of honey on the counter? I don't think it is, but apparently, Carol fucking thinks it is. So, I had to go rooting about in the cupboards, pulling out every jar and shoving my nose in it to see if I had the right jar. I don't know why you'd keep anything other than honey in the house.

God, I love honey.

By the time Carol woke, I had given up my search of the cupboards and sat myself on the floor with the refrigerator open, shoving whatever I could find into my mouth. I was so hungry. I know it's unusual to devour a cold stick of butter, but you try walking around town in the middle of the night with everyone staring at you or running away. Sometimes, butter makes everything better.

It'd been a full minute since Carol appeared at the bottom

of the stairs, and she kept screaming the entire time. One big, loud, ear-piercing scream. I couldn't take it anymore.

Shut up! I roared.

She was scared in the first place. She always is. But I watched the terror form in her eyes, and I felt a little bad about that. I hate being the bad guy, but God, Carol. Just once, could we not do this same song and dance? I have to do that enough at work with all the kids.

I wish, with all my heart, I knew what made her act this way. It seemed so unnecessary, especially since we play out this same scene every time.

"BEAR!" she shouted, pointing at me. "IT'S BACK!"

Sigh.

HUMAN! I roared. *STILL SURPRISED FOR SOME REASON, 'CAUSE SHE'S A STUPID!*

I jammed the last of the butter into my mouth, licked my paw clean, and got up onto all fours. We were going to have a talk right now about her attitude. I paid as much as she did for the right to be here—which is to say we paid nothing; she got it in an inheritance. I showed up the first time as they read the will in the living room, but I digress.

I approached Carol, but she skirted around the kitchen island, keeping it between us, before bolting out the door—and looking quite frightened at the mess I had made of the door. But really, Carol, what did you expect? I'm a fucking bear.

She ran out onto the front porch, screaming about how there was a bear in her house. It was kind of rude, if you ask me. I don't go screaming into the crowds when someone slips into my pen. People frown on that.

Because, one more time, I'm a fucking bear.

At this point, I'm annoyed. I spend my time locked up behind bars. They feed me for other people's amusement. Kids and parents roam through, point at me, and say, "Look, it's Basil the Bear!" and they're all happy to see me. Do you know how hard it is to be on all the time as an entertainer? It wears on you. Sometimes, all I want is to come back to a home that isn't mine— after tricking a small child into letting me out of my pen and eating that child's head—and have some honey without this bitch, Carol, making a federal case out of it.

Is that too much to ask?

I think not.

So, I followed her out to the porch. I know you're not supposed to go to bed angry or follow someone if you're a bear. It's my mistake, and things got out of hand. That's my bad, okay? I admit that.

She turns around and screams again.

I had enough.

Shouldn't have followed, I know, but I did, so here we are as I land a jab to her jaw, following it up with an uppercut through the cleavage. Could have left it at that, but the old Basil the Boxing Bear routine came to the surface—it's like when I was Basil the Bicycling Bear in the circus; once you start on that bike again, it's like a habit that never died. So, I did some of the fancy foot work that always wowed the crowds and then dropkicked her. Wrestling-style, not the football-style. It was an illegal move in boxing, but no one ever complained on account of me being a bear and biting people's heads off.

Carol's now sobbing on her porch like last time, and I feel bad. Once a boxing bear, always a boxing bear. I figure she could use someone to look at the wounds. I'm no doctor. I tried once, but everyone in the emergency room was like everyone else, "Oh, God, there's a bear in here! There's not supposed to be a bear in here! Someone make the bear not be in here!" So, I never became Basil the Brain Surgeon Bear, but I did eat the guy's head. So, he doesn't need a doctor any more … strictly speaking.

But I digress again. I'm so bad at staying on point when

telling a story. Probably something to do with being a bear.

Anyway, so I grab her by the hair and fling her down the porch stairs. I'd considered picking her up by the throat, but I'd spoken with this tiger named Montecore once and whoo-boy is that a bad idea. Something about ripping his friend's throat out. Major faux pas. Humans are so fragile. Stupid, squishy humans.

By now, the neighbors have come out of their homes. They're standing and staring, pointing at us.

So embarrassing.

I wish we could have one time where the neighbors don't have to see us like this. I wave at Fred, trying to act nonchalant. Good guy, left his barbecue unattended a couple incidents ago. He makes a mean bratwurst. Fred gets creeped out by a bear looking directly at him and waving. It's so hard to make friends, I tell you. I roar, try to tell him Carol's been a stupid again, but he just retreats into his home. Maybe he's just nervous about social interaction?

I don't know.

Anyway, I grab Carol by the hair and start whipping her around again. She tries curling up in a ball for protection. Good on her. Probably a smart move given that I'm a bear. I'm doing what bears do.

Someone was on point this time, because the cops show up within minutes of this starting. A van from the zoo is close behind. They come prepared this time, standing up as tall as they can to make themselves look bigger in order to scare me, and I tell you, for a moment, it worked.

Oh, shit, big people! I roared before regaining my composure.

I fling Carol one last time, right into the side of the cop car, and then charge the cops. Next thing you know, I've bitten off one of the badges, backhanded one of them, dropped a flying elbow on the other. It's a real fiasco; I should probably see someone about my behavior. Carol tries getting away, but I leap on top of her and start just … just mauling. No technique, just gnawing and pawing at her.

My bad.

Finally, Linda from the zoo gets her shit together and starts pelting me with tranquilizer darts. It takes a few of them; I've built up kind of a resistance. I heard they're working on a semi-automatic version to pump the darts out quicker. Politicians are complaining about it, and too right they are. It's unsporting, if you ask me.

Anyhow, the darts take effect; I take a nice nap and wake up in the zoo. They rushed Carol to the hospital. So, thankfully, she's safe and recovering.

I mean, for now. This'll happen again. Because, as we've established …

I'm. A. Fucking. Bear.

***

For more information on this author, visit:
@The_0s1s — Twitter

SPECIAL DELIVERY
D.W. VOGEL

I held the female's hand in mine, her soft pink skin hot against my cool green scales. "That's it. Push! You're doing so well."

She squeezed harder with each contraction. I wiped her sweaty forehead and gave her an ice chip to suck between the ripples of pain.

"Just a little more. You can do it," I encouraged her, and she smiled through gritted teeth.

Humans had such a hard time giving birth. My last clutch of eggs hardly caused me a moment's discomfort, but these creatures had babies that barely fit through their birth canals. The smell of her blood made my nostrils flare.

We had received their distress call in deep space. Their home planet destroyed, these were the last remnants of their species, hurriedly shipped away from their doomed world. They hoped to find sanctuary, somewhere to breed and survive so their kind did not disappear from the universe. But their spacecraft proved inadequate, and they were adrift, powerless, light years from any habitable planet.

We arrived just in time.

I brushed her hair away from her eyes. "It won't be long now. Just one more good push and that sweet baby will be here."

We tried to make the birthing room as comfortable as possible. The female reclined on a soft bed with overstuffed pillows. The walls gleamed in spotless steel, but we had planted some of the seeds they brought with them, and familiar plants grew in pots all around. Our ship rocketed toward our homeworld where the humans would be welcome.

My medical training never prepared me to deliver such sweet

little pink babies, but since I was the first to train my lips to make the odd sounds these humans used as language, I became their primary caretaker. Over the months we had traveled, I had come to love them dearly. They sensed that and responded to my efforts.

She grunted and squeezed my hand as the contraction hit her.

"Yes, that's it. Push! Push!"

And a shrill cry pierced the room, painful to my sensitive sound membranes.

I cleaned the baby off and cut the cord that attached it to the female. Wrapping it in a warm blanket, I laid it on her stomach and wiped up the mess of delivery.

"It's a girl," I told her, curling my emerald lips into the expression humans used when they were happy.

"She's so beautiful," the female said, her eyes alight. They forgot the agony of birth so quickly. It allowed them to keep having babies despite the pain.

"Yes, she's beautiful," I agreed. "Such a precious little thing."

The delivery bed had wheels, and I pushed the mother and child out of the birthing room. The baby was nursing already, an excellent sign.

"What a strong baby. She's hungry. She'll grow so fast." I patted the female's shoulder.

The mother beamed up at me from the bed.

We reached the elevator, and I pressed my palm into the identity pad. We descended in companionable silence.

When the doors slid open, I pushed her bed down the hall toward the large bays where her people were quartered. Our ship was never meant to house so many for so long, and when we found these hundreds of doomed refugees, we had to retrofit our holding bays to fit them all in. The humans crowded around us as we entered the first bay.

"Oh, Sandra, she's so beautiful," one female exclaimed.

A male pushed through the crowd. His eyes lit up when he saw the mother and baby. "Oh, honey. Thank God you're all right. Let me see her."

The female handed him the baby, which he picked up as if the little thing were made of glass.

"Support her head," I advised him. "Keep her nice and warm. Her mother will need as much rest as she can get. It wasn't an easy delivery, but that sweet baby is worth it."

The mother smiled at me and squeezed my hand again.

I helped her into her own bed, one of many folding cots we had set up in the bay. The humans had to take turns sleeping because we didn't have enough for each of them, but they didn't seem to mind.

One of them approached me. "How much longer until we get there?"

"We were quite a ways out when we found you," I answered. "We're still months from home. But don't worry. The elders will be thrilled to see you when we arrive. There's plenty of room on our planet for you."

The male sighed and nodded.

"We can never repay the debt we owe you. Our ship was lost. If you hadn't found us when you did …" he trailed off.

"I know. And I'm so glad we heard your call. The elders can't wait for you to arrive."

I patted the new mother fondly and leaned in to press my lips against the baby's soft head. I breathed in the warm aroma of her fresh, clean skin and purred happily in my throat.

This was the fourth baby born since we rescued the humans. I hoped there would be more before we landed. I couldn't be sure I'd still be in charge of the humans' care once we reached our homeworld and the elders took charge. But I had no doubt these humans would continue to breed and flourish under our care.

Our husbandry skills were the best in the galaxy, and the elders would love these humans just as I did.

I licked my lips, savoring the sweet flavor of the baby's skin. My stomach rumbled in hunger.

Yes, we will take excellent care of these soft humans. They are so delicate, so delectable. And the babies are so very sweet.

***

For more information on this author, visit:
wendyvogelbooks.com

STOPLIGHT
M.R. WARD

Jeremy Higgins reluctantly obeyed the traffic light and stopped short of the solid white line. He eyeballed the clock on the dashboard and then glowered into the rearview mirror. The wooden coffin lay silent, deceitfully peaceful. There was just enough time to reach the crematorium and unload the cargo before *the change* happened, at least according to Roger.

Roger Storley was what they called an exterminator and had been doing this job for a little over a year. He rode shotgun and quietly read the obituaries while puffing a cigar. His jeans squeaked against the leather interior as he shifted his weight and flicked ashes onto the floorboard.

Jeremy peeked at the pages and counted a dozen names before retracting his glare to the stoplight. His first day as a transporter had him sweating bullets, but the pay was phenomenal. He could easily afford to move into his own apartment after a couple of months, and then he could find a less stressful job without the concern of beating the clock, but for now he would do whatever he had to do in order to get out of his parents' basement.

The crosswalk light flashed, allowing three huddled pedestrians—two businessmen toting leather briefcases and a woman sipping a Starbucks coffee—to traverse to the other side. The crossers scampered in front of the hearse, which had once been an ambulance, and veered from the vehicle. The man in the blue suit diverted his attention across the street, while the man in black glanced towards the vehicle and increased his pace. The woman's eyebrows furrowed into a frightful pose as she snapped a selfie before continuing to the curb.

Two young women in a baby-blue convertible stopped to his left and lowered their radio's volume. Jeremy watched as the girls whispered and giggled in his direction. He closed his cracked window to dissipate any cackles they might expel. He wasn't in the mood to answer questions or endure snide remarks.

A white van halted behind them, and Jeremy scrunched deeper into his seat. He felt the whole world gawking at him but focused his eyes on the stoplight and the free cars racing to their destinations.

Eight minutes before *the change*. The light at 5th and Elm maintained its stance longer than expected. Jeremy's stomach churned with anticipation.

"Come on," he muttered, looking from the light to the clock to the incessant red light.

"Take it easy," Roger said nonchalantly. "There's plenty of time to unload the body before the change. The crematorium is just around the next block."

Jeremy craned his neck to ensure the security of the casket. Four strands of chains were taut around the timber and strapped together in the center by two hefty padlocks.

The intersection lights switched to yellow with seven minutes to spare, sending a wave of relief over Jeremy's nerves. He readjusted his position, ready to speed around the final block and unload Mr. Dotson, but the rotation skipped the northbound lane and gave the cars on the opposite side of the crossroads a green light out of sequence.

Jeremy smacked the steering wheel and felt his blood pressure spike. "Are you fucking kidding me?"

Roger didn't seem to notice the outburst. He was glued to the comics section, chuckling to himself.

A raspy gasp escaped the closed box, and the chains began to rattle as Mr. Dotson rejoined the land of the living, but he was no longer the jolly fellow his family would have remembered.

Gone were the days of burials and open caskets. Mourners now held memorial services long after their loved ones were nothing more than a pile of ashes.

This was the new normal: transporters and exterminators racing to deliver the dead into cremation chambers within the first hour of death to avoid *the change.*

A board from the top splintered and burst, and the cadaver's moans and grunts filled the cabin, sending goosebumps up Jeremy's spine. Cold fists pounded against the fractured pine, and the chains holding the coffin together clattered violently in response.

Jeremy's heart assaulted his chest as his breathing escalated. Roger sighed, folded his newspaper, and snuffed the cigar on the sole of his black boot. Sweat dripped into Jeremy's left eye. He rubbed the burning organ and tightly wrung the steering wheel. The air conditioner blew furiously but provided little relief to his flushed system.

Roger grabbed the flamethrower hidden beside his seat and climbed into the hull. Jeremy's eyes widened at the sight of Mr. Dotson's purple face peering through the splinters, attempting to squeeze his head through the opening, his creamy eyes searching the air.

The traffic light rotation skipped the northbound lane again, and Jeremy, too terrified to utter a word, screamed profanities in his head and rigorously shook the steering wheel.

"Go open the back doors," Roger said, preparing his weapon.

"What?"

"We're gonna have to do this here."

"You can't be serious."

"We don't have a choice. Either this wood's defective or that is one strong mutha—"

"Okay, okay," Jeremy said and grudgingly opened the door.

A purple cross with white borders accented each side panel and both rear doors of the black vehicle. Jeremy whispered "Please, God" over and over as he walked around the automobile. The girls in the convertible locked their doors despite having their roof lowered. The white van blared its horn, but Jeremy ignored the protest and released the double doors.

"Okay, now go turn on your lights and edge out into the intersection," Roger said, gazing hypnotically at the small flame from the propane torch.

The cadaver punctured another board and freed its right arm. Jeremy turned on the flashing purple lights, started the siren, and crept into the intersection. Motorists simultaneously screeched to a halt. Some honked their horns while others screamed vulgarities from their windows, but all fell silent when Roger expelled the casket onto the asphalt as the hearse rolled to the other side of the street. The box cracked upon impact, but Roger immediately pounced in the middle of the crossroads next to the emerging corpse. He lowered his black sunglasses over his eyes and incinerated the coffin.

A few of the motorists exited their vehicles to get a better look, while others locked their doors and whispered urgent prayers.

After parking the hearse across the way, Jeremy rushed to Roger's side and gawked as Mr. Dotson's flesh melted from his bones. Roger relented once the cadaver was nothing more than a smudge on the pavement. He flashed his teeth under a shit-eating grin, switched off his tank, and lit another cigar.

Jeremy vomited, and then the northbound light turned green.

***

For more information on this author, visit: mrwardauthor.com

PARENTING FOR SEX ADDICTS
CHASE WEBSTER

We are not the type of people who need an occasion to try. That's what they call it, too. Trying. As if the very idea of it is taxing. It's not taxing, and we are not those people.

No. We do not live by some magical calendar. Schedules aren't our thing in general. That's too much organization. It's too stuffy. Too—I don't know—too planned. We're not the type of people who plan.

We can't.

If we could—plan, our lives would be much different, I think. Of course, it's hard to say because this is how we've always been.

Our very togetherness is a result of impulse. The time it took us to decide to move in together was significantly shorter than the time it took us to remember each other's names. In fact, our first conversation happened only moments after the first time we … well. What I mean to say is we didn't plan. Because planning would have been much too stifling for either of us.

It went, "God, that was great!"

Then it became, "We should probably get a bigger place."

And, "I agree."

Before long, we're in this three-bedroom duplex that looks like it escaped Brazil's Favela. In a blink of an eye, I've gone from bachelor, the envy of my friends, living in a Southside on Lamar studio with the only true view of the Dallas skyline, to this … floor cluttered in toys, spoiled milk left out on the kitchen table—again—and the constant chatter of *Bubble Guppies*, or *Minnie's Bowtique*, or *Vampirina*. It all depends on who has my remote.

I had this beautiful human Yin-Yang portrait in my living

room. Like *Shades of Grey*. Very classy. It's in a box now … closeted forever. And instead, I'm surrounded by milestone achievements, like a participation placard for soccer. Not even a trophy. They didn't give out trophies this year because nobody wants to single out any of the kids for being inadequate. This is a God's-honest framed piece of paper that says congratulations for participating. "Good job, honey … You showed up!"

This adorns our living room wall next to finger paintings and family photos and abysmal Mother's Day macaroni-art pieces that I made myself because our three children were either too young or too mature to make anything themselves. I'm a macaroni artist now. Because my photography has been deemed too inappropriate to display in front of the children. Because the words "tasteful" and "nude" apparently have no place together in the same sentence. Because some psychologist told us that we need to wait for our children to be older to—I don't know—fill them in, I guess.

Point being, we don't have time for schedules or occasions. My wife walks by, and the house is to ourselves; the littlest is sleeping cozily in her room. The oldest is doing, God-knows-what with God-knows-who, and our middle child, the star soccer player, is out of sight, out of mind, learning calculus or chemistry or Texas history or whatever it is they teach third graders these days. And the way my wife looks in her sweatpants and dingy brown shirt—may have been white at some point, who knows— well, it's enough. We're knocking formula to the floor and kicking aside chew toys that either belong to our dog or our daughter, and my wife is sitting in the kitchen sink—as good a place as any. She tears the blinds down overlooking our fantastic view of a covered parking lot. Nails dig into my back, and she yanks my hair, and she bites my ear.

No candles. No music. No mood.

She just happened by, and I figured, I guess, three girls isn't enough. Maybe ... by some miracle ... I might have a boy in me this time.

Which brings me to the half-day. Someone cold and hateful invented it. Because normal school hours are too much. Because six hours of school with four fifteen-minute breaks and one whole hour for lunch is too much. Four uninterrupted hours of learning a day is somehow too much. And my daughter, for all her hard work, gets this occasional three-hour day that she somehow neglects to tell us about. Every. Single. Time.

Our neighbors also have a third-grader. Thomas. Sometimes Kayla rides with them. Nice folks. Mormons, I think.

Yeah, well, I forgot to lock the door, and Kayla, my little princess, decided to let everyone in. I'm sure you can imagine their surprise.

***

For more information on this author, visit: chasemwebster.com

BUTTERCREAM MARJORIES
TRAVIS WEST ⚡

Danny turned at the sign reading *Maplebrook Winery and Vineyard* and steered the car down a rock driveway. A gift shop and a big red barn greeted visitors inside of whitewashed wooden gates. Beyond the gift shop and barn was a much larger and utilitarian-looking building which served as the vat-house.

"How's the wine in this place?" asked Jim from the passenger seat.

"No idea. Marjorie's friend Camille booked the place. But trust me, if the wine was crap, Camille would not have brought Marjorie here. The lady definitely knows her stuff."

"Camille," Jim said, letting the name roll off his tongue. "Is this Camille single?"

Danny smiled. "As a matter of fact, Camille is very single. Not only is she single, she's Marjorie's maid of honor, so you two get to walk down the aisle together."

"Nice. Height?"

"Guessing, I'd say five-seven."

"Hair?"

"Shoulder length, wavy but not curly, and auburn."

"Birth defects?"

"Birth defects? What the hell, man?" Danny laughed. "No, none I've ever noticed."

They drove around the side of the barn and to the short strip of parking spaces along the side of the vat-house. To the left of the building were rows of red grapes. To the right, white grapes. Between the two was a small meadow of short grass, henbit, and wild violets.

The meadow extended over one hundred yards to a dense

wooded area, the trees close enough to keep sunlight from breaking through. The width from red grapes to green grapes was nearly eighty feet. Peppered throughout the meadow was an innumerable amount of women in bridal dresses. None of them stood more than four feet from another. None of the dresses were the same, coming in a multitude of shades, hues, and cuts. They all, to the woman, faced the trees at the far end of the meadow, still as statues with their arms raised in the familiar bouquet-holding position.

The only movement came from a string quintet halfway down the right edge of the meadow. Danny shut off the car to listen and recognized their song: Cyndi Lauper's "True Colors."

"Dude," Jim whispered. "This is the weirdest bridal shower I have ever seen."

Danny nodded. "Maybe they're almost done? They should have had it wrapped by now." He checked his watch. "Marjorie said four o'clock. It's only three-fifty; we're just early."

The two men exited the car and walked around the back of the vat-house. They approached the edge of the meadow, stopping short out of deference to the silent women.

"Danny, you're here."

Both men turned around.

Marjorie stood beneath a latticed archway of the type used for outdoor weddings. She wore a silver wedding gown, form-fitting and sparkling in the late afternoon sun. In front of her was a microphone stand, the cord trailing to the building. Her voice had boomed from speakers; although, he could not see them anywhere.

"What is all this?" Danny asked, unable to quell the awe in his voice. "Marjorie, you are—you look—Wow."

Marjorie smiled, her cheeks flushed.

"I brought Jim," he said. "I was thinking we could introduce him to Camille." He looked around the vineyard. "Where is she?"

Marjorie belched, loud and long. A breeze blew through the meadow, bringing a honeyed aroma reminiscent of, but not quite, vanilla.

"It's buttercream," Marjorie exclaimed, bouncing on her heels in excitement. "I hope you don't mind, Danny, but I've decided on a buttercream assortment for the wedding. It's all so wonderful. I've sampled spiced butter cake, with buttercream icing, of course. The finest butter-mints, which were delectable."

"That's a lot of butter," Danny said, feeling delirious and drunk on the sugary fragrance emanating from his fiancé.

"Uh-huh. Hot buttered rum, buttered Camille, and even a—"

"Wait, wait," Danny said, interrupting her. "You accidentally said Camille. Where is she again?"

Still smiling, Marjorie moved her hand in a circle across her belly. She ran her tongue in a cartoonish fashion around her lips, making an exaggerated slurping sound.

"Danny, you're here."

Danny turned around to face Marjorie. Another Marjorie, in another dress. The quintet began another song. "Kiss the Bride" by Elton John.

"Danny, let's forget the big to-do and get married now, here."

"Back off, you," Marjorie One said. A shadow darkened the sparkle in her eyes, and for a moment, Danny thought he saw movement beneath the skin of her face—writhing, knotted, and serpentine. Then the illusion of transparency passed.

Marjorie One swung her bouquet, striking Marjorie Two in the face. A thorn from a rose tore into her cheek, drawing a thick pus-like fluid.

The sweetness in the air intensified.

Buttercream, Danny thought. *It's buttercream.*

Marjorie Two grinned, turning Danny's stomach. Every

tooth in her mouth was a molar, front to back—not a single incisor or bicuspid in sight. "What makes you so special? I want him more."

Marjorie One growled, reared back for momentum, and shoved Marjorie Two with all her might, sending her doppelgänger crashing into the back of a third bride, who slammed into a fourth.

All the remaining women in the meadow issued a collective gasp and turned to face the commotion. They were all a Marjorie. Some had red hair, others were brunette, but they were all Marjorie.

The dispute between One and Two spread like an angry cancer. Shouts of "He's mine," "Keep your hands off of him," and "I saw him first" reverberated around the meadow as the Marjories fought, punched, and clawed each other for their prize.

The quintet played on with growing fervor. They lost their hats, revealing musical Marjories.

"What happened?" Danny asked. "Where's *my* Marjorie?" He pointed to Marjorie One. "What is that?"

Jim, looking horrified, shook his head. "A succubus?"

A curly-haired Marjorie broke from the swarm and approached Jim. "What did you say, cutie? I'll suck your bus."

Another Marjorie grabbed a handful of her hair, yanking her back to the fray and tearing a section of scalp as she did so.

"Danny." Jim, his voice barely a whisper. "Danny, we've gotta get out of here. I think they ate your friend Camille. Maybe even Marjorie. Let's get to the car and go."

The smell of buttercream permeated everything, and Danny struggled against impending unconsciousness. He reached for the microphone stand as his knees buckled, but it was no use. Unable to get his hands in place to break his fall, he landed squarely on his chest and chin, knocking the wind from his lungs. Feedback from the fallen microphone squelched and groaned from the hidden speakers.

Every Marjorie stopped where she stood and faced the two men at the archway. The altar.

"Danny," Jim said. "Stand up. On three, we haul ass to the car. Okay?"

Slowly, Danny rose to his feet.

The Marjories all took one step forward with their right legs. They were drooling, and every left hand rose to wipe mouths clean. Danny thought of bird murmurations and schools of fish.

The Marjorie quintet kept playing.

"One," Jim whispered. "Two."

Releasing a unified war cry, the Marjories charged forward.

***

For more information on this author, visit:
facebook.com/TravisWestWrites

THE SURPRISE ⚡
GENA WHITE

Nick placed the Tiffany-like box on the porch. The teal package screamed, "I miss you, I want you back."

Three months earlier, Nick had left work early to take Shelly to her favourite restaurant—the one of their first date. He could remember it like it was yesterday. The night before, he had laid awake in bed wondering why the woman of his dreams had accepted to go on a date with him. Him, the beer-guzzling, long-haired bum who thought a night at Bill's Tavern was fancy. How could a woman like her be interested in a thing like him? But she had been, and the date turned into many. He ditched the leather and long hair for a three-piece suit and a ten-dollar cut from the local barbershop. Within months, she had him whipped, but he didn't mind, she was happy. This was until he found her, spread eagle with their mailman delivering his package.

He placed the card under the blue ribbon for safety measures and took a step back to admire his surprise.

He strolled by the park on his way back home whistling to The Beatles' "Run for Your Life," jogged up three flights of stairs, hung his keys, and hopped out of his shoes. He shimmied over to the fridge like Fred Astaire and grabbed a six-pack; his other hand clutched a bag of pretzels. Then, his boogie feet brought him to his laptop; he flipped it open. The old thing made more noise than a Boeing 777, but he was broke after spending all that cash on his surprise. A page popped up; he entered his username and password. A smaller pop-up screen appeared in the left corner.

"And now, we wait." He grabbed a beer, chugged it, and shoved a few pretzels in his mouth. "This'll be better than a movie," he cheered as crumbs fell on his shirt.

The clock showed 1 a.m. *She should be home by now.* Was she still with him? Earlier, from the bushes, he had watched as a pile of muscle opened the passenger door to a compensating-for-something, piece-of-shit car. What the hell was she thinking hooking up with that loser?

His indexes drummed on the desk. Her surprise would not wait. Too bad he could not be there to yell "Surprise!" but she had to be alone to fully appreciate his effort. She complained about how he was not creative enough; this would change her mind.

The dark square on the laptop became a dim glow, the image was grainy but bright enough for him to see her delicate arms pull the teddy bear out of the box. She hugged the plushy and gazed into its eyes.

Nick gasped, but the camera concealed in the left eye went unnoticed.

Had she read the note? He squinted. Tears covered her cheeks. Sparks filled his stomach. Her tears broke his heart even more than her past actions. *This is a mistake. I shouldn't have, but she cheated, and now she needs to pay.*

This had been easier when her face was a memory. The clock above the sofa read 1:53. He looked at the receipt. *2:05 a.m.* was written in black marker—the predicted time of his surprise. He still had time. He could stop this nonsense.

He grabbed his cellphone and tried to call but remembered she had blocked him. There was no time to get to the house. Nick looked around. His heart raced. He crumbled the receipt and threw it at the screen.

"Shit," he barked. "Shit, shit, shit."

His eyes refocused on the screen. Shelly stood. Her arms reached her waist, and her t-shirt rose. His eyes grew larger. Nothing in the world would make him look away. He had not seen her body in weeks. For a moment, he forgot all about the surprise. He missed her soft skin and the way she smelled like orange blossoms. His fingers shook, touched the screen, and outlined her image.

He scanned the right corner of his screen—1:59. Maybe it wouldn't work. Customer service mentioned a slight chance it would fail. He would win her back, and everything would be normal again.

She climbed into bed and grabbed an object. Nick looked closer—a picture frame containing a photo of them at the beach. She kept a picture of them by her bed? He wiped his clammy forehead. Nick stood and placed his face inches from the screen as she spoke to the bear. He tried to read her lips. Did she know he was watching? Nick made out the word "sorry" as mascara-coloured tears cascaded over her cheeks and chin.

"Maybe it won't work," he whispered to the screen.

But as soon as the clock turned 2:05, it happened. Shelly howled as millions of baby spiders hatched out of the teddy bear's belly. They crawled over her satin sheets and her naked body, turning everything black in their path.

Legs, hairy bodies, and black beady arachnid eyes invaded the camera lens. Nick's view changed to vanity chair legs and the spider swarmed carpet. He placed his head sideways. He could see her in the distance; her arms flayed from side to side like a mad air controller. She fought, stomped, and slapped pin-sized spiders as they took tiny bites out of her sweet, scrumptious, orange blossom-scented body.

Arms stretched out, she grabbed the bear, her face twisted in shocked as she spotted the camera. She took two steps backwards, caught the foot of the bed, and tumbled, bringing the bear with her. Her head bounced off and shattered a ceramic wiener dog doorstop to pieces. Blood splattered on the white door and on the spider-infested carpet. A trickle of blood streamed out her gaped mouth as lifeless eyes stared at Nick.

His plan had worked. She would never cheat again.

***

For more information on this author, visit:
facebook.com/Genawhiteauthor

PLEASE DON'T KILL ME
RAYONA LOVELY WILSON

"You're staring again," Nate says, sliding onto the stool across from me.

He's the reason I get up in the morning, the reason I breathe. He's so damn cute, the way his black hair is perfectly slicked back.

"Sorry. You're so perfect." When we're together, he sparks a fire in me.

"I'm not perfect," he says. He said the same thing the first time we met at a nightclub downtown. "We need to have a talk."

"Okay."

His deep-sea-green eyes remind me of the time I went snorkeling with my parents years before they died. I get lost in those eyes, almost like his soul is sucking me in. It's the only place I'm comfortable, the only place I'm wanted.

His lips move, but I don't hear what he's saying. Those lips I've grown so used to kissing make it hard to focus. He reaches across the tiny round table and touches my shoulder, sending butterflies through my stomach. We're soulmates.

"I should go."

"What? No. I thought we were spending the day together," I say and grab his hand off my shoulder and intertwine our fingers. "You promised."

He's all I have here. If we're not together, my mind goes crazy.

"Ash, this is exactly what I'm talking about. I want to be able to do things without you, but you're so ... fuckin' clingy," he says and yanks away his hand and places both in his lap under the table. "I can't do this anymore."

"What? Come on, Nate. We're fine."

He glances out the window, and I notice a hooded figure across the street. Do they know each other?

"Did you not hear anything I said a few minutes ago? I swear you don't listen to me. I cheated on you! I'll spell it out for you: I—had—sex—with—somebody—else. It was meant to make you not want to be with me."

Cheated? He wouldn't do that to me.

"You're such a liar. Why don't we go back to my place and—"

"Damn it, Ash. You don't get it!" he says as he stands, grabs his phone, and marches out the coffee shop.

Is he serious?

"Order twenty-nine, your raspberry iced tea is ready."

That's Nate's. He orders the same thing every time we come here. I grab it from the counter and leave.

He's walking toward his apartment with the hooded figure, but I can't see who it is. Is that who he cheated with? Does he not remember the countless nights we've spent together? That must mean something to him.

He pulled me from a dark place after my parents died. He can't end things like this.

They stop outside his apartment. I try to give them their space, but I need to hear what they are saying. They don't see me as I crouch in the doorway of another complex. What the hell is he thinking?

The person in the hood heads down the street, and Nate looks around before opening the gate to his apartment. Now's my chance.

I run to the gate before it closes, trying not to spill any tea as I slide in my hand.

He stops walking. "Oh my God, Ash. What are you doing?"

I hold out the tea. "You forgot your drink. You paid for it, and I wanted you to have it."

He folds his arms across his chest. "You expect me to believe you came all this way to give me my drink? Try again."

Why is he angry?

"I can't live without you. Before we got together, you know how bad off I was. I can't go back to that. I have nobody else," I say as I step toward him again. "You and I belong together." He's seriously all I have in this world. "My biggest fear is being alone. I told you that when we first met."

"I'm with you all the time, and it feels—I feel—like you're suffocating me."

I can't help but let out a laugh that shakes my entire body. Because I'm suffocating him, he slept with somebody?

"It's okay. We—we can fix it. Let's forget about it and move on."

"No. Come get your things. We're done."

I stare at him, at the tattoos peeking from the collar of his shirt. I want to touch him so damn bad.

"Okay."

We walk down the hallway to his apartment, and I drop the tea in the trash. His hand brushes against mine. I try to link our fingers, but he stuffs his hand into his pocket.

"Sorry."

I'm not sorry; he's my boyfriend.

He sticks the key into the lock and shoves open the door because it often sticks. I follow him inside and close it. I love being locked in here with him, watching horror movies all night long.

"I put your stuff in a box over there," he says, pointing across the room, and then approaches the fold-out couch we've sat on so many times together.

I can't believe he expects me to take my stuff and move on with my life. I have no life without him.

Instead of going to the box, I walk to where he sits and stand right in front of him. "Nate? I can't live without you."

"Yes, you can."

I can't help but fall into his lap, straddling him.

"Ash, please st—"

I don't give him time to finish his sentence, because I press my mouth onto his, slipping my tongue between his teeth.

"What—Ash, no," he protests and grabs my hands, yanking them from the button of his pants. "I'm done with you."

"But you're so hard right now."

I lean forward and kiss him again, even though the position he's holding me in hurts my arms. He can hurt me all he wants as long as we're together.

"I slept—Ash, I slept with a girl. I told you I wanted to experiment with you, see if I really had feelings for a guy, but you made me realize I don't."

He lets my wrists go, and I can't help but stare at him.

I touch his face, the scruff I love so much now prickly under my fingers. "We haven't—we never even had sex. You liked everything I did to you."

"I know, but … I don't feel for you like I do Brittany. That's who you saw me with."

He doesn't mean this. He's told me I've made him feel out of this world. How does he feel nothing for me after these last three months?

"Don't cry."

He rubs my arm, attempting to comfort me, but it's not working, not now. He promised he'd never see a girl while he was with me. How could he lie?

"You should go." His voice is a whisper.

"No. You made me better; you made me want to live," I reply and pull his face to me, placing my lips on his warm ones. "Please, don't kill me."

He pushes me to my feet and stands. "I'm sorry. Go clean

yourself up and grab your stuff."

He leads me to the bathroom, gently pushing me inside.

When the door closes, I stand in front of the medicine cabinet, staring at myself in the cracked mirror. I knew I'd never be good enough. Why'd he have to experiment with me? I open the medicine cabinet, and rows of pills fill my vision. I told him I can't return to what I was before him, and I meant it. Vicodin and sleeping pills should do the trick. I grab the two bottles and turn on the faucet. That asshole cheated on me with a Brittany? I grab his mouthwash cup and fill it with water. Nate Miller doesn't get to cheat on me then end our relationship. I pour the Vicodin into my hand and stare at them. If I survive, he'll want to be with me, and if I die, he's the cause. I throw them in my mouth and drink the water, nearly choking as they hit the back of my throat. I should've taken them one at a time.

"Ash, you alright in there?"

No. I'm not. He promised he'd never hurt me. I hate him like I hate my parents for leaving me alone the night they died. I throw a few sleeping pills in my mouth at a time, not wanting to think about my parents.

"Ash …"

Shit. My heart slams into my chest, and I look at the now empty bottles. Do I really want to die? I should have been stronger.

You're so worth it. That's what Nate had said, and he lied. He made me feel special at one point, and now I'm nothing.

"Dude, what are—oh my God!"

I hear his distant voice, feel his hands on my shoulders, and smile. I wanted him to want me so bad, and now …

***

For more information on this author, visit:
facebook.com/shewhoscribbles

THE COOK ⚡
AARON WULF ⚡

The cook tested the rib meat one more time for tenderness and returned the stew to a simmer. She leaned her back against the granite countertop, checked her watch twice, and drummed with her fingertips.

It was 9:15 p.m. Her husband had been upstairs for three hours now.

She checked five cabinets until she found what she was looking for and poured herself half a glass of Chateau Lafite Rothschild 2009. She relaxed again and sipped it slowly.

The kitchen was dark, all except for soft LED lighting strung above the cupboards. The faint sound of a radio played by the fridge. She went to it and turned the volume up.

"... *have new leads. The only information we have right now is that they are armed and very dangerous. We know that there are two suspects, and the last confirmed murder was late last night. The victim's name has not yet been released, but we know he was a senior at Pinegrove High School. Go Falcons.*" The DJ cleared his throat. "*We urge all of you in the Pinegrove area to please stay inside and lock your doors. Police are working overtime to catch the serial killers, and just moments ago, the police chief said that they are closing in on their trail. We here at WHAF just hope and pray that the murderers are caught before they kill again. That's it for the news buzz. My name is DJ Buzzkill, and you're listening to WHAF, The Drop. Now begins our all request hour. Here's the song 'Familiar Taste of Poison' by Halestorm, requested by me. Keep it real, you buzz maniacs.*"

The cook didn't move. She breathed in slowly, paused, then exhaled. She closed her eyes and listened to the beautifully haunting melody on the radio.

"Baby?" she called.

No answer. Nothing in the house moved but the bubbling stew.

She made her way through the kitchen and into the laundry room. She drew back the sunflower-print curtains and looked out the window. It was just an empty backyard with a swing set.

She then made her way to the dull-lit living room. She peeked through dusty window blinds, but all she saw was the moonlit snow and their '04 Chevy Blazer in the drive sitting next to a snow-covered Escalade.

The singer on the radio drifted into the first chorus when the deep hallways of the house echoed with a sharp pang.

The cook froze, still holding her glass of wine, and shifting her weight from the right to the left. She peered down the hallway. "Babe, you there?"

No answer again.

She placed her glass on the coffee table and looked down at her belly. It was bigger than it had been two months ago. She caressed it with her fingers, smiling.

She slowly stepped into the hall when the bang happened again, this time louder. It was coming from the basement.

Her heartbeat quickened; sweat beaded on her forehead.

"Hun, if you're not downstairs in two minutes, I just might lose my shit. I don't know how much longer I can do this." She said this quietly, more so to herself than to anyone who might have been listening.

There was a table against the wall just across from the bannister. Above it hung a giant mirror with a brass frame and roaring lion faces on each corner. On the table was a lamp, a few decorative boxes with brass latches, and family portraits.

She picked up a picture—a mother, a father, and two beautiful girls. The girls were twins, and both had long blonde hair like their mother and round faces like their father. In the picture, the family sat in a grassy meadow with autumn trees in the backdrop, and a picnic spread before them.

The cook smiled, caressing the glass where the girls both laughed.

The girl on the left had a yin-yang necklace, which was tangled up with her sister's heart-shaped locket.

She removed her hand from the picture, placed it on her bump, and sighed. "I promise you, someday everything will be normal."

Glass shattered downstairs.

"Oh god," she said.

Tomorrow's news headline played in her mind like a marquee: *PINEGROVE MURDERERS STRIKE AGAIN.*

She returned the picture frame to the table with a solid clunk and continued to the basement. Once down the stairs, she turned the corner to the left, following the finished basement around in a *U* shape and stopped at a giant deep freezer.

Behind the unplugged freezer was a white door, braced not just with the freezer but with two 2x4s sitting on makeshift hooks.

The cook put her back against the appliance and shoved it away. She then lifted both planks off the door frame, set them aside, and unlocked the door with a twist and ping of the handle.

The cook stiffened.

The putrid stench made her nose scrunch.

The room was dark, cold, and small, but the street lamps from outside shined through a tiny window up high.

The windowpane was shattered. Only jagged slivers of glass remained. Blood dripped from some of them, and a small heart-shaped locket swung loosely from a shard.

In the back of the room, half hidden in shadow, crouched a blonde woman holding a broken piece of glass in her right hand. Short frayed strands of rope lay on the concrete next to her bare feet.

"What do you think you're doing?" the cook asked, unfaltering.

The blonde woman didn't speak. In her left hand she held a phone. The screen read *9-1-1*.

A distant voice from the phone spoke: *"The police are on their way. Please stay on the line."*

Crouched on the floor next to the blonde woman was a little blonde girl, hands still tied behind her back with rope. Her yin-yang necklace hung from her bruised neck.

"You down here?" a familiar male voice said somewhere near the stairs, causing the cook to start. "What the fuck's going on?"

"They called for help," said the cook.

"You were supposed to check for phones. Where's the other girl?" asked the cook's husband, looking over her shoulder into the dank room.

The cook stared up at the open window. "She's gone. But she's hurt, she won't get far."

"Good," said the husband. "Easy dinner."

The cook said nothing. She stood still, arms wrapped around her belly, looking down at the little teary-eyed girl.

"Kill them," the husband said. "We can't stay here any longer." The man reached under the Pinegrove letterman jacket he wore and pulled out a pistol. "Take care of it."

"It hasn't gotten easier," she said, taking the gun in a trembling hand.

"It will get easier, trust me."

"No, it won't."

"It's us or them. Do it."

"I don't know if I can anymore. The baby." She faced him, eyes welling with tears.

He cupped her cheek in his warm hand and kissed her cold, dry lips. "This is our future. Be strong, or we both die."

"What if I refuse?"

His face turned to stone. "Then you'll die. I'll be sure of it." He turned, then paused for a moment and said again, "Take care of it," then he walked away.

The blonde woman and the girl were both crying, shaking, and holding each other close.

The cell phone was no longer in the mother's hand but on the floor. The screen no longer said 9-1-1. It had gone black.

"Be quiet," whispered the cook. She closed her eyes and took a deep breath. After a few seconds, her eyes opened. She stepped over the mangled heap which had been causing the acrid smell and aimed the pistol. "I'm sorry," she said.

One shot pierced the air, and for seconds, she only heard a ring. She opened her eyes and saw the shot was true. She fired another deafening blow.

The room was quiet and smelled like rotting eggs, rotting cabbage, and feces. Smoke flowed from the barrel of the gun.

She dropped the pistol and left the room, stepping over a body. This body belonged to a man. He was long dead. Dried blood stained the floor around his torso, and his ribs had been removed.

Just two inches above where the mother and daughter had been crouched, two clean bullet holes smoked from the drywall.

A crisp January breeze filtered in through the window, carrying with it the smell of short-rib stew. The heart locket clinked against broken glass.

Soon, the dead man was the only thing left in the room. Upstairs, the song on the radio reached its end, and the tires of the '04 Blazer squealed off into the night.

DAISY CHAINS
CAROLYN YOUNG

"He loves me, he loves me not," the girls chanted as they carefully picked the petals from a daisy flower. Sitting in a circle with their legs crossed, the rough grass itching against their bare legs, they giggled as one of the girls ended in, "He loves me not."

Sarah stood, her eyes stinging with disappointment as the circle reformed, excluding her. She looked toward the huge weeping willow near the school fence line, the curtain of leaves shifting in the wind. He waited there. She knew it. But she hadn't been selected today. *He loved her not.*

She quietly walked away, watching from a distance as the remaining girls picked their next flower and resumed their chanting.

Only a few days had passed since they'd started this ritual. When *he* started at the school. All the girls wanted to be with *him*, not just because *he* was the new guy. *He* had a way of making everyone feel special, as if no one else held *his* interest. They would fight for the chance to date *him*, before someone— she couldn't remember who—had suggested the daisy competition. It was the obvious solution. They couldn't all be with the same guy, no matter how gorgeous *he* was, with *his* dark hair and piercing eyes. When they told *him* about it, *he* looked them up and down, smirked, and agreed. The daisy competition meant they each had a chance to be with *him* for a day. So far, Sarah hadn't been the lucky one.

Her friend Jane had been chosen yesterday. Sarah imagined herself in her friend's place, holding his hand with her clammy one, gazing into those dark piercing eyes, becoming lost in them as they stole their first kiss. She'd been looking forward to finding out from Jane what to expect, but Jane was away sick today, so she couldn't ask. Pangs of jealousy warred with curiosity. She wanted to know, she didn't want to know.

Sitting in the shade, Sarah heard the girls arguing. Someone had cheated. They'd picked off two petals at once. The girls pushed the offender from the circle, with another "love her not" girl, and turned their backs to continue their game. Only three remained now. "He loves me, he loves me not."

The final three girls, their flushed faces visible even at a distance, picked their next flower. None were Sarah's friends, but she wanted to watch to the end to see who was chosen.

The chanting began. "He loves me, he loves me not." Finally, an audible gasp erupted from the winner who stood unsteadily, looking from the remaining girls to the tree where her prize hid. It was Lauren. She took a few slow steps toward the tree, looking backward at her friends, then lifted her chin and marched through the curtain of trailing leaves.

They all looked away and headed in different directions as if no longer interested in Lauren's actions. They'd all return tomorrow for another go.

The following day, Jane and Lauren were absent from school, but the rest of the girls still formed a circle, picked their flowers, and chanted, "He loves me, he loves me not."

Damien stood behind the tree, awaiting the victor, and whispered quietly to himself, "I'll eat you, I'll eat you not," as he gnawed the meat off a bone.

"He loves me." Sarah's heart skipped a beat as she realized it was her turn.

She turned her back on the other girls, wiping her sweaty hands down the front of her dress, and stepped behind the tree. She reached to take Damien's hand, stealing one last look at the retreating girls as she felt his cold, sharp dagger pierce her heart.

The last thing she heard before she lost consciousness was

Damien's voice whispering, "I'll eat you."

***

For more information on this author, visit:
facebook.com/authorcarolynyoung

CPSIA information can be obtained
at www.ICGtesting.com
Printed in the USA
LVHW091909030219
606250LV00001B/3/P